"Midnight. Church bells rocking in the bitter winter air cried out a joyful welcome to the new century...Happy New Year! Happy 1900!"

As the little village of Aurora celebrates the beginning of a brand-new year, Jen McAlister doesn't realize 1900 will be quite a special year for her and her family. This is the year she turns fourteen, the year she discovers talents of her own as well as learning some ugly family secrets from the past. But most amazing of all to Jen, she discovers the pleasures and pains of a first love.

By the time the McAlister family gathers for their Christmas dinner in 1900, we have indeed shared a very special year.

To Meta Hawley Perez
who was there

PUFFIN BOOKS
Viking Penguin Inc., 40 West 23rd Street, New York, New York 10010, U.S.A.
Penguin Books Ltd, Harmondsworth, Middlesex, England
Penguin Books Australia Ltd, Ringwood, Victoria, Australia
Penguin Books Canada Limited, 2801 John Street, Markham, Ontario, Canada L3R 1B4
Penguin Books (N.Z.) Ltd, 182–190 Wairau Road, Auckland 10, New Zealand

First published by Houghton Mifflin Company 1985
Published in Puffin Books 1987
Copyright © N. A. Perez, 1985
All rights reserved
Printed in the United States of America by
Offset Paperback Mfrs., Inc.,
Dallas, Pennsylvania
Set in Plantin

Library of Congress Cataloging in Publication Data
Perez, Norah A.   One special year.
Summary: Chronicles the adventures of Jen and her family
in turn-of-the century upstate New York.
[1. New York (State)—Fiction] I. Title.
[PZ7.P4260n 1987]   [Fic]   86-30378   ISBN 0-14-032202-7

One Special Year

N. A. Perez

Puffin Books

Contents

To the young each season holds its chores and its
enchantments.
If spring is a cheeky blaze of dandelions and pleasuring mud
it can also provoke a rabid female craziness that loonily
snaps at a child
and sends it out attacking carpets with a stick.
Summer is swinging flight above the river on a flimsy rope
and waiting for the gold-and-scarlet circus wagon to
roll in along the dusty tracks of August,
but it is also endless weeding in a kitchen garden
and tiresome lawns to cut.
Autumn? The snap of apples, chestnuts hoarded like satin
wampum, and a mocking October kicking up more leaves
to rake.
Then comes the time to hold the hard metallic blade of winter
dangerously in hand,
to skate topspeed over rubber pond ice and hurtle downhill
on a pair of barrel staves;
it is knowing that in the polar body of December
thumps the warm red heart of Christmas,
and it is filling the woodbox again and again.

FROM THE NOTEBOOK OF LUKE McALISTER
AURORA, 1900

1

The Bells Ring at Midnight

Midnight. Church bells rocking in the bitter winter air cried out a joyful welcome to the brand new century.

"Three . . . four . . . five . . ." Louisa McAlister counted.

Jen could tell her mother was anxious about her best crystal as she handed around the cider.

"Six . . . seven . . . eight . . ." chanted Charles and Maybelle.

"Nine . . . ten . . . eleven . . ." Everyone joined in: Papa, checking the time by his gold pocket watch, Luke and Jen, and Gram, wide awake in polka dots.

"Twelve! Happy New Year! Happy 1900!" Smiling, the family members turned to each other, carefully touching the fragile goblets together as bubbles rushed upward in bright, foaming sparks. Jen saw her father set his aside. Taking his wife's face gently in his hands, he kissed her. Quickly she turned her cheek, her fingers reaching up to brush his touch away.

"Nineteen hundred!" Gram held out her empty glass for more. "I never thought that I'd live to walk around in another century."

"And I never doubted it for a minute." This time the

man's kiss stayed put. All of them were crowded in around the woodstove in the kitchen, but as its glow warmed their faces, a chill climbed up their backsides. Mama brought out the Lady Baltimore cake from the pantry but Papa said, "First let's each give welcome to this special New Year."

Luke, seventeen and handsome in his dark red robe, bowed to his parents and raised his glass again. "To Mama, then . . . may she bake many more Happy New Year cakes. To Papa . . ." Jen saw a mocking flash in her brother's long blue eyes. "May he drink many more convivial toasts. To Gram, Jen, Maybelle and Charles . . . may we always remain as loving and united as we are tonight."

"Thank you, son. Those are fine words." His mother looked at him with pride and satisfaction, and Jen envied Luke's ability to say what Mama wanted most to hear. "Let us drink to our good health." Mama only pretended to sip as she didn't care much for the taste of cider. Lightly she touched Charles on the forehead; the eight-year-old boy had been running a fever since supper.

"I think we should pray." Maybelle, at ten, was a great deal preoccupied with praying, and Jen hoped that the new century would cure her of it.

"Later, my dear." Gram's glass was empty again. "Let's not spoil the fun just yet. How about a toast to all the good times ahead?"

"And to poor Aunt Ella!" In his excitement Charles spilled cider down his nightshirt, and everyone thought of young Ella Landers, newly widowed and on her way to them from Pittsburgh. Not *really* an aunt. Jen was sure that there was some mystery about her that no one would discuss.

In the sudden quiet interval Louisa McAlister glanced at her thirteen-year-old daughter. "I'm sure Jen has something worthwhile to contribute."

Everyone turned, glasses held high as the girl drew her black brows together in thought.

> *"Good-bye, dear eighteen ninety-nine,*
> *The year we've just been through.*
> *Too bad we had to kick you out*
> *To make room for the new."*

There was laughter. Luke winked and Gram gave a hearty sideways poke to show she was amused, but Jen, seeing the disappointment in her mother's face, felt the sad inner knock she always experienced whenever she let her down. Mama had such high expectations; she seldom saw the funny side of things. She had hoped for something serious or sentimental to mark the special event, and now Jen would have to wait another hundred years to make amends. Yet she had only wanted to recapture the good feelings all of them had shared before Ella Landers was mentioned. Flustered, she turned to her father. "I know Papa has something important to say."

"I do happen to have a few words on hand." Light from the hanging kerosene lamp shone on Jamie McAlister's thick black hair and lustrous groomed mustache as he fumbled for his notes in the pocket of his waistcoat. Luke winked again, but Jen avoided meeting his eyes. She never liked his making fun of their father, especially in the bored, superior way he did it these days. Papa did have an impressive way with words, the gift of gab Gram called it.

"As we gaze out eagerly upon the new century," he began, "we do not merely hope for the best, we *expect* it." His voice was resonant and mellow. "The last one hundred years have seen this great nation grow to upwards of seventy-five million inhabitants. Think of it! We are now the world's leading industrial power. Two great oceans have been linked by a transcontinental railroad. Every day we hear of wonderful new inventions that will benefit mankind. One day electric lights, telephones, even automobiles will be commonplace here in the village of Aurora. This is an age of confidence, of boundless optimism! It is to the glorious future that I propose my toast. And may you all live happily in an era of peace, prosperity, and progress — for many years to come."

Jen, moved by her father's speech, clapped her hands enthusiastically. How handsome and clever he was, with the right words for every occasion. Why was Luke smiling so strangely as he set down his empty glass?

"Now may we pray?" Maybelle was eager for the limelight.

"Hurry up and do it, love," Gram said. "And then, let's eat!"

2

The Arrival

It was the middle of the afternoon when brother and sister started for the depot. Jen was glad to escape. She had been polishing brass for hours. "Why bother?" she always asked. "It just gets tarnished all over again."

"When you're married and have a home of your own, then you'll know why," was the answer she always got. "And if you can't do a thing cheerfully, then don't bother doing it at all." So all morning Jen had bashed away at doorknobs and candlesticks, lamps and andirons and trivets, even the dented old spittoon that her grandfather Hiram had once hit with legendary accuracy and that was now kept glowing in his memory.

Charles had begged to go with them but had been kept in with a feverish cold, and Maybelle had been needed to do other chores. Their house, a faded frame with front and back porches added on, was a mile from the village; a freezing walk on a windy January day with a fine gritty snow slashing down. They walked quickly and in silence, Luke's cap pulled low over his moody eyes and Jen's red scarf snapping in the breeze as they hurried down the road along the river. Once they would have chattered all the way, for they had been close friends in a childhood that Jen remembered as one long sunny summer afternoon. Then Luke had never minded having her around. They had played kick-the-can and Civil War in the cemetery and searched for the dark red hearts in the Queen Anne's lace that foamed across the meadows. When a line of children had played crack-the-whip, Luke had allowed her to be last, guaranteed to whirl into space at the speed of light — until she'd sprained a wrist that way and her mother had firmly put a stop to it. He'd shared his *American Boy's Handy Book*, as well, with its useful instructions for making armed war kites and other ingenious things, and the forbidden adventure stories in *Pluck and Luck* that had to be hidden from Mama because she thought they were such trash. When had it changed between them? Jen thought it must have been five years ago when Ella ran away to Pittsburgh to be married. After that Mama took sick and seemed oddly locked away in her mind. A terrible time.

"When you get to the end of your rope, tie a knot and hang on," Mama said, but even as her health improved things were different. Luke was distant. He spent his evenings alone in his room, reading late into the night and scribbling things that no one was allowed to see, and Jen felt shut out.

By the time they reached Aurora, her fingers and toes were numb with the cold. They passed the *Echo* office, the First Commercial Bank, the barbershop with its red-and-white-striped pole. All the businesses in the Brick Block were closed on New Year's Day. "Let's stop in at the store to get warm," she said. Their father had left the house early in the morning to check over his inventory.

The front door of McAlister's was locked. Jen, peering in through the ice-frosted window, could see no sign of life within. "Maybe Papa's in the storeroom at the back."

"You didn't really think he'd be *here*, did you?" Luke kept on walking. "Hurry up, or we'll be late for the train."

Farther down Main Street one place was always open for business. A confusion of male voices roared out of Dewey's saloon. In church, the minister often lectured husbands about wasting money on liquor while anxious wives and hungry children waited at home, and yet Jen, hearing the noisy laughter and the cheerful clink of glasses, inhaling the golden scent of ale, always felt a guilty curiosity as she passed by. Even though her mother detested the place, Jen wished that just once she could enter that mysterious domain where no respectable woman would dare to be seen.

From the door of the tavern a voice called after them, "Come back here, you two! I want to wish you a Happy New Year!" It was Thomas O'Connell, an attorney and Papa's best and oldest friend. He kissed Jen and reached out to shake her brother's hand. "I've just been talking to your father about you, son. Would you have a few minutes to discuss something with me?"

"We have to meet the four o'clock train, Mr. O'Connell," Luke told him. "Ella Landers is coming here today from Pittsburgh."

"So I've heard. Well, your New Year won't be dull with

Ella in it." The lawyer's eyes were dark and amused in his long, pale face. "Then will you stop in at my office one of these days? I may have something to say that will interest you."

"Yes, sir. I'll do that."

There was a piercing thrill of sound in the distance that sent a rush of excitement through the girl. "We'd better run!"

"Jen, wait a minute." The man's long, slender fingers seized her ear and gently tugged. A small paper sack appeared in his hand and he dropped it into hers. "Chocolate creams, young lady. Your mother's favorites, I believe."

"Thank you, Mr. O'Connell." She smiled at him. "Oh, I wish that I could do that trick!"

"Sleight of hand, my dear . . . and sometimes very useful to an attorney." He waved them on their way. "Off you go!"

The train whistle shrieked again as they ran along the slippery street toward the depot. Quickly they scrambled over some high, dirty snowbanks and dropped down into the railroad yard below. There were usually a few idlers hanging around the freight office waiting for something to happen, but with the sun sliding low and the temperature plunging below zero there was no one in sight, not even Mr. Diebold from the livery stable with the promised horse and cutter. Moments later a locomotive burst from behind the stationhouse, scarlet coaches rattling along the tracks as the hissing engine screeched to a stop. A uniformed conductor swung down and helped a small woman dressed in black alight upon the platform. Jen, arms wide open, ran across the hard-packed snow to greet her.

"Oh, my!" Ella breathed, hugging her. "Jen, dear — you've grown so tall! And Lukas, let me look at you. A man already, and such a handsome one at that. I just cannot believe my eyes."

"You haven't changed, Aunt Ella." But Jen thought that the fair crinkled hair, the light blue eyes and summery skin were even lovelier than she remembered. Yes, and she recalled the delightful habit the woman had of addressing all males, old or young, by their formal given names.

"You needn't call me aunt, you know . . . we aren't kin."

"Mama says we ought to show respect."

Ella took their hands in hers and squeezed them tightly. "You can respect me when I'm old and gray . . . *if* I deserve it."

"Well, then . . ." Shyly Luke touched his reddened cheek to hers and dabbed on a kiss. "Welcome home, Ella."

"And we're very sorry about your . . . Mr. Landers." Jen was anxious to get that over with.

"You have no idea what a shock it was," Ella said. "Toppling over the way he did in a barbershop. A stroke, poor man . . . and just a month before Christmas."

The cutter had arrived, the lean horse shuddering and sending feathers of vapor out through his nostrils. Mr. Diebold slouched behind the reins, his rheumy eyes screwed up small against the cold. He grunted at them, juggling a lump of tobacco from one jaw to the other while Luke handed up the luggage and helped Ella to a seat. A jet of steam shot out from under the wheels of the train as the cars slowly clattered away along the tracks.

"It's so good to be home again," Ella told them, "but I don't want to be a nuisance to anyone. I'll try not to be in the way."

Jen tucked a heavy buffalo robe across their knees. "We have plenty of room." Luke had already moved downstairs into the little office space where generations of McAlister men had kept the bookkeeping records for the general store.

"It isn't the room, dear . . . it's the imposition. But there's simply no place else for me to go. Everything in Pittsburgh had to be sold off to pay Leland's debts. *Gambling debts*," she whispered, so that Mr. Diebold wouldn't overhear. "Your mother was right about him after all. If only I had listened! Why, these mourning clothes aren't even paid for." She touched the flared brim of the hat that framed her animated face. "Isn't it awful to have to spend money for ugly things you absolutely hate to wear?"

She looked about with interest as the horse moved away through the dim, brisk air. Some ragged children stood staring at them boldly from high on a frozen drift and then sent a shower of snowballs smashing after the cutter. "There, you see?" Ella said. "Just when I think I'm badly off and start feeling sorry for myself . . . Well, take a look at those miserable little creatures."

Mr. Diebold swore fiercely under his breath. "Them bloody Claffins," he muttered. "I'd like to wring the necks of every one of 'em."

"You people here don't know how lucky you are," Ella

said. "Once you've seen the real world — lived in a big city — then your whole outlook changes. I've seen little boys not much older than Charles doing a man's job in the iron mills for twenty-five cents a day — why, that's inhuman! And girls your age, Jen — slaving away from dawn until dark trying to keep body and soul pinned together." She drew her arms through theirs, pulling them closer for warmth. "Now you must catch me up on all the news. Your mother hardly ever wrote."

"Mama's ashamed of her handwriting," Jen said. "Leaving school early the way she did."

"Jen, that's nonsense. She could have written upside down for all I cared, as long as I heard about all of you. You've finished high school, Lukas?"

"Yes, I'm working at the store."

"I remember when Louisa had her heart set on you becoming a clergyman."

"Mama has her heart set on lots of things," Luke murmured, "but I was never interested in that."

The cutter whirled around a corner and turned into Main Street, the runners rasping on the crusted ice as the horse danced past the livery stable, Gentle's Blacksmith Shop, the bright green façade of Pickwick Hall.

"Nothing has changed — it's all the same!" Ella cried, as they glided past Roth's Meat Market, Miss Phair's Millinery Establishment, the general store with *McAlister's* in gold on the frosted pane. "I suppose your father's still handing out credit to one and all?"

"Yes, and Mama says we'll all go to the poorhouse one day, wherever that is," Jen said.

"Louisa's a practical woman, and thank goodness for that. James never did like keeping books. He's such a romantic."

"Romantic?" Jen laughed at the idea. "Papa's thirty-seven years old, Ella. What's romantic about that?"

"Pooh, that's not so old! Mature men are always more fascinating than younger ones. My Leland was fifty-one and in his prime, vigorous and lively until the day he died." A spot of pink burned at the tip of Ella's nose. They had left the Brick Block behind, and the sleigh bells clashed in the tingling air as the cutter raced homeward along the River Road. Where the crisp land dipped they caught glimpses of green water, blistered with ice floes, moving swiftly in the direction of Lake Tuscarora. Here and there they passed handsome big houses, shuttered for the winter, with vast lawns blank with snow. Only in summer did those frozen estates come to life, with striped awnings shading deep verandahs and tea parties tinkling in the graceful gazebos. Jen always thought with longing of the basket carriages and ponies belonging to the pampered children of the very rich.

"Lukas?" Ella touched a hand to her bright hair and becoming hat. "How do I look? I want to be at my best for your mother."

His cheeks blushed even redder than before. "You look all right."

He could have sounded more enthusiastic, Jen thought. He'd hardly spoken a word since they had left the depot. Wasn't it obvious that Ella Landers was the most beautiful woman he had ever laid eyes on?

3

A Homecoming Dinner

Ella tapped her water goblet with a spoon. "I just want to thank you for letting me stay here for a while and to tell you how happy I am that we're all together again."

Mama, seated nearest to the kitchen, looked as if she were afraid that Ella would overflow as she had done at the drop of a hat when she was small. Tears alarmed her; Jen had never seen her mother cry.

Charles spoke up. "We're not *all* together. Papa's not home."

"I'll fetch some hot gravy." Quickly his mother rose and left the room.

"Now why did you have to bring that up?" Maybelle's big hairbows trembled with indignation. "Can't you see she's upset about it?"

"He'll be here any minute." Jen passed warm baking-powder biscuits on to Gram. "He was probably held up at the store." But if he had stopped in at the tavern, it might be hours before he got home. Then Mama would be angry, and Ella's homecoming spoiled. Worry was a tight knot in her chest.

"I can't wait to see James!" Ella said.

Supper had been laid out ceremoniously in the dining room. It was a festive meal, as elaborate as any Sunday dinner. There was the best sprigged pink-and-white Limoges china with curliques of faded gold and a snowy cutwork cloth that Mama never allowed anyone else to iron. She didn't care at all about fashionable new things, but she did treasure the few fine heirlooms that had been handed down in the family — a pair of Sandwich glass candlesticks, a sterling berry spoon, some delicate fragments of old linen. Tonight she had stuffed and roasted a chicken, set out a mound of mashed potatoes and a steaming casserole of squash (not a favorite with the children) because she had remembered Ella's fondness for it. There was corn relish and watermelon pickles, and on the dark walnut sideboard two kinds of pie for dessert, warm mincemeat in a fluted crust and apple, with a graceful A pricked out in pastry.

Maybelle, who had delivered a lengthy grace resplendent with many *Thees* and *Thous*, had been staring raptly at the guest of honor ever since. "Aunt Ella," she said, "we have missed the two great events in your life."

"Whatever happened to the gravy?" Gram peered over the top of her eyeglasses. She had a hearty appetite and said that she liked to take care of her victuals at mealtime and let the conversation take care of itself.

"Mama's getting some hot from the kitchen." Jen turned to her sister. "What great events are you talking about?"

"The trouble with Louisa," Gram continued, "is that she never gives a fellow a fair chance to eat. Hopping up and down, popping in and out, snatching up dishes before they even have a chance to settle — why, a body has to be some sort of an acrobat in order not to starve."

"You love Mama's cooking!" Charles, delighted by his grandmother's outburst, knew it was not to be taken seriously.

"I'd enjoy it even more if I didn't have to tackle it midair." Gram took hold of a dish of crabapple jelly and held on for dear life.

"Why, the wedding and the funeral, of course," Maybelle went on, as if there hadn't been an interruption. "We kept the clippings that you sent us from the newspaper, Aunt Ella. In fact, I know them all by heart." Rapidly she quoted:

> "*A wedding of unusual brilliance was celebrated in the parlors of the Great Western Hotel when Miss Ella Cordelia Wingate and Mr. Leland L. Landers were married yesterday. The ceremony was performed at five in the afternoon in the presence of an assembly of relatives and friends. The Reverend George Thorburne, pastor at First Congregational Church, officiated.*"

Maybelle caught her breath and plunged on.

> "*The bride and groom were unattended, but as they took their places beneath a beautiful canopy of foliage, the enchanting strains of the wedding march were heard. Miss Parthenia Croops presided at the piano.*"

"Presided!" Ella laughed, and then began to choke, her shoulders shaking as she took a sip of water. "Overpowered it would be more accurate. Parthenia positively assaulted that shaky little instrument with such a passion . . . Well, it sounded like Hannibal thundering over the Alps."

"Who's Hannibal?"

"He had elephants, Charles." Maybelle put a finger to her lips. "Now shush, you."

"Like a circus? At Aunt Ella's wedding?"

"No, Charles, there were definitely no elephants." Ella blotted her eyes with her napkin, smiling at them through her sparkling lashes. "Maybelle, didn't that clipping mention the flowers? The smilax and asparagus fern and the big wedding bell made out of red and white carnations?"

"Never mind the flowers," Luke said. "Just tell us what you had to eat." With his thick, curly hair standing up around his head he looked like one of the stained-glass saints in the windows of St. John's, but Jen wasn't taken in. His mocking eyes were making fun of Ella, and anyone could see that she was as trusting and gullible as a child.

"That was in the papers, too," Maybelle told him. "Bluepoint oysters, soup, and salmon royale, and stuffed chicken breasts with truffles."

"Truffles?"

"Charles, don't you know anything? Pigs sniff around in the dirt and dig up these queer little things that are very delicious and extremely expensive."

"Well, I know one thing," the boy said, and laughed. "I wouldn't eat anything some dirty old pig dug up. I guess I'm glad I missed that wedding."

"Oh, Charles . . ." Ella smiled. "It really was magnificent. We had champagne with every course."

"That's a fine sparkling wine," Maybelle rushed to explain. "But if you pull out the cork wrong you can blast out an eye."

"There were no casualties," Ella reassured them.

"I'm sure it was a charming affair." Mama had taken her place again at the table, her deepset eyes more blue than gray in her excitement. She was wearing a starched shirtwaist, its high stiffened collar fastened with a cameo brooch. "A woman never forgets her wedding day."

"Do men?" Charles wanted to know.

"Men aren't that keen about weddings," Ella told him, "but it's the most important day in a woman's life."

Gram nudged Jen. "Would you kindly pass along that gravy boat before it sails away again forever?"

"Your husband is dead now, so you can have another wedding, can't you, Aunt Ella?" Charles asked.

"That is not polite!" Mama spoke sharply. "Mr. Landers only died a few weeks ago."

"Well, he can't hear me."

"Tell us about your wedding, Mama," Luke said, and Jen noticed the quick soft look his mother gave him.

"There's nothing much to tell, son."

"You said a woman never forgets."

"I didn't say I'd forgotten . . . It was a very quiet affair, that's all."

"Please," Jen said. "We'd really like to know."

Perhaps if they could distract her long enough there would still be time for Papa to arrive before dessert was served.

4

Mama Remembers

"We didn't have many guests. Jamie's parents — " Mama smiled at Gram — "my father, a few relatives, and Ella, of course. She was just a tiny girl." She glanced shyly around the table, surprised to see them all staring at her. "We were married at Wilson's Corners in my front parlor on a Saturday in May. I remember how cheerful and yellow the forsythia was and that beautiful red tulips were blooming all around the house."

"And I was the flower girl," Ella suddenly remembered.

"I'll say you were." Gram chuckled as she reached for another biscuit. "You picked every blessed one of those pretty tulips and sold them to the wedding guests for a penny apiece. That's when I knew that you'd get on in life!"

"Go on, Mama." It was rare for her mother to glance back into the dusty corners of the past; Jen was afraid she might stop talking.

"After we spoke our vows we ate a bit of supper, and then Jamie and I took the late train to Rochester to visit an aunt."

"An aunt!" Jen was astonished. "Why would you do a thing like that on your honeymoon?"

"It was my old Aunt Rose, and to tell you the truth I never liked her that well. But she invited us, and it was someplace else to go. We didn't have any money, not for hotels or that kind of fuss. It was all we could do just to scare up the fare. Jamie wasn't keen on it, either . . . but I suppose I talked him into it."

"Yes, you always had that boy of mine wrapped tight around your little finger," Gram said, but kindly.

"Why didn't you just stay home?" Jen asked.

"I was too . . . embarrassed."

"Newlyweds are like that," Ella agreed. "So skittish and so nervous. At our wedding reception I could hardly eat a bite."

"No wonder!" Charles banged his fork down on the table. "Truffles — no wonder!"

"There was nothing wrong with Leland's appetite, though. He took second helpings of everything."

"He was entitled, wasn't he?" Luke was still making fun. "After all, it was his second wedding."

Suddenly everyone was talking and laughing, and once again Ella was the center of attention. Jen leaned closer to her mother and asked softly, "Were you very happy on your wedding day?"

After a long silence Mama answered. "I was afraid."

"Afraid?"

"I remember how hot it was . . . I was sitting alone in that stuffy parlor waiting for the guests to arrive, and it was so quiet I could hear my blue silk dress rustling and the sound of my heart beating so quickly." She paused again, her thumbnail making little worried imprints on the tablecloth. "I thought I might be making a terrible mistake."

"But why?" Jen asked. "Weren't you madly in love?"

"Jen, of course not! That's only in silly novels. But I must have been bewitched." Mama's voice was just a shade above a whisper. "Jamie was a charming boy. And how he loved to sing in that sweet voice of his . . . and whistle . . . and dance. And the way that he recited poetry!" Jen knew his waltzing Irish way with words, how he could rattle off rhymes by the line, the stanza, the minute, the mile. "And wild for fun, he was . . . how he could laugh! Yet he wasn't all nonsense, either," Mama went on. "No, I never would have stood for that. He had a steady quiet side as well, and he was hardworking when he wanted to be."

"Then why did you feel afraid?"

Laughter and conversation went on around them, and Jen realized that her mother was sharing something very private just with her.

"It all happened so fast. I was just seventeen and that's too young. But your father wanted me for his bride, and I wanted to get away, so I gave in."

"Get away from what?"

Mama didn't answer that. She said, "I felt so breathless on that day."

"The way you do on holidays?" Jen, feeling a familiar pained sympathy, put her warm, square fingers over her mother's hand.

"Yes, like that." Abruptly Mama pulled away. She never wanted to be touched. After all her happy effort, her genuine pleasure in Ella's homecoming, Jen saw that Mama needed to escape, throw open the windows and doors, draw in a breath of fresh air. "Your father won't be coming now." She stood up and asked, "Is everyone ready for dessert?"

Across the table Ella laughed at something Gram had said. Again Jen thought how beautiful she was with her warm summer glow lighting up the cool, wintry room. Maybe Ella would let her paint a portrait of her soon. Not in that dress, though. Black was the color of mourning. Ella was life!

"Pretty Girl?"

It was Papa's voice, loud on the other side of the wall.

Silence.

"Dear, 'm sorry. Stayed in town longer'n should have. Could'n be helped."

There was no reply.

"Know you're awake . . . lying there all tensed up like that." The voice stumbled on, "Say you're not mad. Please, don' be angry with me."

Jen, lying beside her sleeping sister, curled her knees up to her chest and wrapped her arms around them.

A shoe dropped. "Lissen . . . brought you something . . . some nice cologne that came into the store this week."

Didn't he know by now that Mama didn't care about gifts, that she could only give and not receive?

The other shoe dropped. "Come on, Pretty Girl. Give

me a kiss. Let me kiss you. I'll make it up to Ella to-morrow."

But Mama would not forgive him soon for staying in town. She might be silent and withdrawn for days, and it was her brooding silence that frightened Jen more than any angry words.

The brass bed creaked. "G' night then, Pretty Girl. Sleep well."

Still there was no reply.

The next room to Jen's was a sad room. She had always sensed that. Why couldn't her mother reach out and hold him the way he wanted to be held? If only she would, then something brittle in the house would break and they could all be happy. Yet she never would. Why was Mama so cold, so unfeeling?

Maybelle made a noise in her sleep. She was grinding her teeth again, driving Jen crazy. Jen wished that she had a place to herself, a bed of her own.

There was no further sound from beyond the wall.

5

A Bell in the Night

Some time in the night the fire bell rang. Jen wakened briefly, then sank again, this time to dream of hats. A summer's day, eloquent with speaking hats, the gentlemen's bowlers and boaters lifting and tipping, and the great confectionary cartwheels on the ladies' heads responding with graceful dips and bows. Sunlight leaned in through the sparkling windows of Miss Phair's Millinery Establishment, illuminating dozens of bonnets, and in the middle a cloud of white, the loveliest one of all.

She remembered the dream in the morning. It made her long for the hazy heat and freedom of summer, the glorious excitement of the Fourth of July. She stood up, relieved that Maybelle had left the room, and began her Madame Bonnomo's Bust Developing Exercises. Clasping her hands in front of her chest, she tugged strenuously in opposite directions. Then she did the brisk arm rotations. She had sent away for the instructions from a newspaper advertisement a few months before, and although Madame Bonnomo had guaranteed a magnificent, full, uplifted bosom, the miraculous results had not yet been achieved.

Quickly Jen stripped off her long flannel nightgown. She would have liked to snatch everything up and make a dash for the kitchen, to dress by the woodstove as she had done as a child, but hurrying now, prickly with chill, she shivered into an undershirt and waist, underpants with broad bands of embroidery at the knees, long black stockings darned at the heels, two petticoats, and her oldest, warmest dress. The floor was frigid beneath her feet. There was even a film of ice in the china basin, but she knew that if she skipped washing up her mother would only send her back to do it properly. Twisting her face against the shock she dabbed freezing water on her cheeks and vigorously scrubbed them dry with a towel. Face glowing, she looked at herself in the oval mirror above the commode.

"You have crazy eyes," Maybelle had jeered more than once. "As if you're laughing at something inside your head."

"Maybe I am!"

"And I'm glad I don't have that awful Injun hair." But Jen knew that her sister envied her straight, waist-length hair, as black as any Tuscarora squaw's. Even Mama, so modest about her own appearance and who seldom commented on anyone else's, called it Jen's crowning glory and insisted that she brush it one hundred strokes every night. She also told her to put lemon juice or vinegar into the rinse water when she washed it, to give it extra shine. Still gazing into the mirror, Jen piled her hair up on top of her head, swaying this way and that, pretending that she was modeling one of Miss Phair's most delectable creations.

"What do you think you're doing?" Charles watched from the doorway.

"Why, can't you tell? I'm trying on my beautiful new spring bonnet."

"Well, I like it." He grinned at her. "That's some hat!"

She laughed, picked up her boots and ran with them, light-footed, down the stairs. The kitchen was fragrant with the rich smell of coffee. Waves of heat radiated from the woodstove where Mama, erect and trim in a starched white apron, stirred the oatmeal. Jen noticed her strained face, the shadows deep beneath her eyes. "I wish I could have some coffee. It smells so good."

"Coffee is for grown-ups, Jen."

"I'm practically fourteen."

"That's not grown-up." Maybelle sat holding a struggling cat in her arms. There was sleep in her eyes, and Jen knew that she hadn't washed her face, but for some reason their mother hadn't noticed. "Aunt Ella is grown-up and Luke almost, but you don't even have stays."

Jen ignored that remark. It wasn't her fault that Mama wouldn't let her wear corsets yet. "Did I hear the fire bell last night?"

"You certainly did," Mama said. "Mr. Riley told us all about it when he brought the milk around this morning. A vagrant, they think, set fire to the livery stable when he was in there trying to get warm. I'm surprised the whole town hasn't gone up in flames before this with all the drinking and gaming that goes on in that wretched place."

Jen was glad that indignation made her mother talkative. "Did Luke go?"

"Yes, and thank goodness the volunteers got the fire out in time. Mr. Riley says there was no great damage."

Jen went to the window and pressed her forehead against the frosted pane. It was still dark outside; soon morning sunlight would touch the rushing water and set the river blazing.

"Mr. Riley said the horses were frightened clear out of their wits," Maybelle reported. "But the firemen covered up their heads with blankets and got them all out safely." Puss escaped from her arms and hid behind the stove. She was a haughty, indifferent cat.

Jen peered downriver where, in bright winter sunshine, the Hotel Eldorado would gleam like a castle of ice. Vast and sprawling, the great white edifice was situated on a high rise above the broad blue vista of the lake. Each year visitors arrived from distant places to amuse themselves with boating and bathing, lawn bowling and tennis, a bicycle gymkhana in July. Mr. Landers had been staying there when he first saw Ella and persuaded her to elope with him. Jen said dreamily, "Someday I'm going to dance at the Eldorado." On soft summer evenings waltz music floated from the hotel ballroom past her window.

"I've no doubt that you will," Mama said, but she *sounded* doubtful. "In the meantime we'll have to do something about your skirts."

"What's the matter with them?"

"The way you've shot up so lately . . . Why you're hardly decent with your dress hiked up like that. We'll have to cover those legs."

"Why? Are they so ugly?"

"Ungainly, Jen. Unladylike. When Warner comes this spring she'll have to let down all your things."

"But how will I run?" Jen wanted to know.

"You'll walk," Mama said.

The trouble with growing up, Jen had discovered lately, was that every new privilege won meant some dear freedom lost. She desperately wanted stays, all of her friends did, but Jessamine Doyle, who had been the first to wear them, said they were the cause of her frequent fainting spells. Jen didn't believe it; she was convinced the girl was simply showing off.

"When I was little I didn't think you had any legs," she told her mother as she laced up her boots. "After all, I've never seen them."

"Then what did you think held me up?"

"I don't know. Wheels, maybe."

"Wheels, is it? I could use some, trying to keep up with the lot of you." Mama poured coffee from the blue enamelware pot on the back of the range, and handed the cup to Jen. "Now hurry up and look in on Mrs. McAlister. She'll be waiting for you."

After all these years Mama still could not call her mother-in-law by any other name.

Jen was glad to go. There was something she intended to ask her grandmother, something she wanted to find out before she left for school.

6

Gram Tells a Secret

She started up the stairs, careful not to spill the coffee. Her grandmother would be waiting in the sloped room under the eaves, easing back and forth in her cane-backed rocker with a yellow shawl crossed over and pinned at her breast.

"I don't like getting in the way in the morning when things are hopping downstairs," she had explained when Jen asked why she didn't eat breakfast with the family. "Not that your mother would mind. It's just something we've worked out between us over the years."

Gram was truly fond of her daughter-in-law. Even though she wished she wouldn't call her Mrs. McAlister, she respected her need to keep that space between them and let it go. "Your Mama and I get along just fine," she had once told Jen. "Of course she has her faults, but I have mine. You can depend on Louisa. And she never lies, not ever."

"Gram?" The old woman sat with her cramped hands held out to the stovepipe that twisted up from below, sending along a crooked message of warmth. "Are you all right?"

"Frozen stiff is what I am." Gram reached eagerly for the coffee. "Good girl. Hand it over."

Puss followed Jen into the room. She had arrived as a stray a few years before but still managed to give the impression she was only passing through. Puss was a temporary name, but even though she had stayed on the name had stuck.

"Get along, you scalawag — I'm not a-moving yet!" Gram's cane-backed rocker was the cat's favorite chair, and when the old woman wasn't in it, the gray cat was. "Back to school today, young lady?"

"I don't mind. I'm even looking forward to it." Jen picked up the crazy quilt from the bed and threw it over her shoulders like a cape. She spun around, taking pleasure in the whirling scraps of brilliant color. "Our class is planning a Box Social for Valentine's Day . . . maybe even a sleigh ride after. But if I have to sit next to Willard Roth I swear I'll die." She tossed the quilt back on the bed and flopped on top of it, swinging her long black legs.

Gram drank greedily, her bumpy fingers clasping the warm china cup. "The butcher's boy? What's the matter with him?"

"Everything. For one thing, he kind of whinnies when he talks. And he always smells of mothballs. And all he ever talks about are natural disasters . . . like volcanoes throwing up or quicksand gulping down the nicest people. My friend Mary Frances says that Willard's a natural disaster."

Gram laughed. She loved all the children, but it was Jen who could tickle her funny bone, and she loved to laugh.

"He keeps pestering me," Jen sighed. "I don't know why he won't leave me alone."

"I guess he knows a good-looking girl when he sees one," her grandmother said.

Jen smiled. She had inveigled a compliment because she wanted to go to school feeling good about herself. All her mother ever said was that a petticoat was showing or that something wanted mending. *A stitch in time saves nine.* How many times had she heard that? What would she do without Gram to give her a lift when she needed it? She was glad that they had come to live in the homestead where McAlisters had lived for generations. Sometimes she wondered how many babies had been brought roaring into life here, how many folks laid out in the parlor with a black mourning ribbon drooping on the door. It had been twelve years since Grandfather Hiram had died and Gram had decided that she couldn't keep the place on her own, that she only wanted to be sleeping next to her husband again. That's when she had asked her son and his family to move in with her. She had given over the house in spirit and in deed, and none of them had ever regretted it. In time she had felt less inclined to move out to the cemetery and had learned to enjoy again the life that hummed around her.

"There's something I have to know," Jen said.

"Ask away."

"When did Ella first come to stay with Mama . . . and why?"

"What does your mother say about that?"

"You know how she is . . . She doesn't say."

"That's because she's always looked out for Ella and

protected her. You know she hates gossip and scandal, and I say good for her, except," Gram said, "these things usually come to light anyway, and sometimes the sooner the better."

"What things?"

"It's time you knew the truth, Jen . . . but to spare your mother's feelings, let's keep it between the two of us. Luke already knows. I told him a long time ago."

"Told him what?"

"That Ella . . ." Gram chuckled softly. "When she was tiny I never saw such a hugging, loving child . . . squeezing everything that she could get her hands on."

"*Gram.*"

"And the way she dragged poor Luke around when he was small, washing his face, combing his curls . . . Remember when I used to call him Buttercup? Like he was a plaything, a little baby doll. I used to tell her she'd wear him out before he had a chance to grow up."

"Gram, will you tell me or not? I'll be late for school if you don't hurry."

"Yes, I'll tell you! Ella's a love child."

"What's that?"

"She was born to a hired girl living on a farm near Wilson's Corners. The girl had no husband, that's the big secret, that's the disgrace. The farmer turned her out, and she came to your Grandfather Wingate for help. He was a minister, but not a charitable man, I am sorry to say. I doubt if he'd have raised a finger to help . . . all he ever did was scold on about sin . . . but Louisa took in both mother and babe and did what she could. Then when the hired girl died of milk fever, Louisa kept the youngster to raise."

"The baby was Ella?"

Gram nodded. "And your mother only fourteen, living in that big, dark house with a harsh father and a helpless infant. Somehow she managed; she always does. And when she married my Jamie a few years later, of course she took Ella with her. That little girl never could do wrong in Louisa's eyes."

Love child. It had an alluring and romantic sound.

"The trouble with Ella," Gram said, "is that she's always done pretty much as she pleased. It took your mother a long time to get over it when she ran off with that Landers fellow. I never want to see her hurt that way again."

All that had happened so long ago. Jen didn't want to hear any more about the trouble with Ella. The impulsive girl of sixteen who had eloped was years older now; surely she had changed.

"Get out of there, Charles! I saw you snooping."

"Was not!"

"Liar. I'm marking that down."

Jen heard the commotion on her way down the hall. Maybelle, her arms folded bossily, stood in the doorway to her parents' room. Lately she had been jotting down sins, not only her own on a rather small list, but her brothers' and sister's on a very large one.

From the bed Papa asked sleepily, "What's going on around here?"

"Charles has been a very bad boy," Maybelle reported. "He's been poking through the things on your dresser and playing with your gold medal, and now he's wearing your boots, and on the wrong feet, too!"

She flounced away, her plaid hair ribbons bouncing.

"Morning, Papa." Jen looked in to see her father sitting up in his nightshirt with his hair standing wildly on end. He looked haggard after his night in town.

"Morning, Papa." Charles smiled delightfully. In his hand was a shoehorn, a lovely polished curve of tortoiseshell that he liked to invert over his nose for the rhinoceros effect. He did like to meddle with his father's possessions: the cigar cutter shaped like a little guillotine that had once almost decapitated his thumb, the scatter of loose coins, the tumbled dice, the tin of mustache pomade. Most of all he liked the small velvet box that sprang open to reveal the gold medal that Papa had won in an oratorical contest in his youth.

Papa got out of bed and hobbled barefoot to the chest of drawers where he picked up a small flask wrapped in leather.

"I'll just rinse out my mouth." It was a thing he always said he planned to do, but never did, for the whiskey went straight down and stayed. His shoulders sagged. Coughing, he slapped himself across the chest while Charles watched with interest as his father punished himself into wakefulness. Then Papa smiled, and held out his arms. "Come here, Charley-boy, and give me a kiss."

The little boy scuffled forward with a laugh.

"Trying to fill the old man's shoes, are you?" Papa picked

up his son and rubbed his mustache affectionately against the boy's red cheek. "Better not try . . . you never know where those big bad boots will lead you."

Charles shrieked as his father tickled him. It gave Jen a queer feeling, remembering how Papa had once hugged and tickled her, too. Now her mother said she was too old for that sort of thing and except for a brief goodnight kiss he seldom touch her. Wistful for a moment, she watched the two of them romping together, and then she turned and left the room.

7

A Visit to McAlister's

"You could give me a hint," Davey said.

"No."

"One little clue?"

"That would be cheating."

Jen walked along Main Street slightly ahead of the tall, broad-shouldered boy. A freezing wind whipped at her heels, flipping up the hem of her coat. Every so often the long red tangle of her scarf blew lightly across his cheek.

"You'll be sorry if I bid on Jessamine's lunch box," he told her.

"So will you. You'll probably get triple indigestion."

Stinging flakes whirled into their faces. His trousers were thickly feathered where he had let her push him into a snowbank. "Jen, come on — tell me!"

"Davey, stop it!" They had reached McAlister's general store. The girl paused and looked up at him, half annoyed and half amused at his persistence. It gave her a strange sensation when his green eyes caught and held her attention. They stared at each other. Something quick and alive behind the warmth of those eyes made her suddenly shy. They had been involved in the teasing argument since leaving the red brick schoolhouse together and had pursued it in and out of drifts and around hitching posts. Now, still hoping to prolong it, the boy blocked her entrance to the store. "You know what those silly Box Socials are like. You end up eating fried chicken with someone you can't stand."

"It isn't me you care about — it's missing out on Mama's Lady Baltimore cake!" Laughing, Jen stamped her feet to keep the circulation going. "Davey, I have to go now."

"Can't I walk you on home?"

"No, my mother wouldn't like it. Besides, I promised to wait here for Ella. It's her first day working in the store." A bell tinkled as Jen opened the door. Hanging kerosene lamps shed a soft yellow light inside. "I really do hope we get to sit together at the social, but I can't break the rules."

"I know." His smile was friendly in his reddened face. He was a tawny-haired, muscular boy of fifteen, older than most of the eighth-graders. He had missed two years of schooling working on his family's farm outside of town. "I was only joking. Anyway, I know you'd rather be partners with Willard Roth."

She made a comical face of dismay. "See you tomorrow."

Going into McAlister's after school was a habit of years. The store was as intimate and dearly familiar as her own house, its smell indefinable, rich and pervasive. She knew where a thousand and one homely items were kept: the penny candy, tobacco, and cigars in shining glass cases to the left, yard goods and ready-mades piled high on wide shelves to the right. There were barrels and boxes and bins, sugar and flour and crackers, a great orange wheel of strong cheddar cheese, an ancient coffee mill, hats and hardware, and in the middle a potbellied stove with chairs on both sides where customers could sit and catch up on the local gossip whenever they dropped by. Everyone in town stopped in at least once a day to pick up the mail and chat with little, bent Miss Hutchins, who could be heard but rarely seen in a tiny, cluttered cubicle at the back. Jen often helped out, dispensing needles and thread, bootlaces and calico, eggs and soap and tea, tying parcels in acres of brown paper and miles of string.

"Goodness, can school be out already?" Ella was sorting embroidery floss behind the counter. "Now I wonder where today has flown?"

"Was that young Sawyer I saw you talking to out front?" Papa was on a ladder piling overshoes on the top shelf. "Looked like a mighty serious conversation."

"It wasn't." Jen smiled up at him as she unwound her scarf.

The doorbell tinkled. Harry Shomers shuffled in, a decrepit hat smashed down around his ears, boots flapping open, the foul wet stump of a cigar dangling from his lower lip. The old man peered into the glass case next to the cash register and pointed. "I'll take that one."

Ella, scattering his smoke with her shapely hands, gave him the last cigar in the box.

"Hah! Got it!" Harry whooped gleefully. "Last one, Jamie! It's for free, ain't it?"

"That's right," Papa said from his perch in the air. "Custom decrees that the last one in the box is free."

Luke had come out of the storeroom and stood with his hands on his hips, listening to the conversation. Jen recognized the look on his face. He was always watching people with those keen, observant eyes. Why? Just to amuse himself, to feel superior?

"Your timing is nothing short of miraculous," Papa told the old man. "To tell the truth, Harry, I don't believe you've had to buy a cigar in here for years."

Mr. Shomers clutched the front of his greasy coat and doubled up with laughter that was almost agonizing. Then he sat down beside the stove and squinted at Jen. "Whatever happened to that cute little black-eyed gel who used to sit in my lap and sing for me?"

"She grew up, Mr. Shomers." Jen held her tingling hands out to the warmth.

"Come on," he coaxed, patting his knee. "Sit here and sing for me again." Tunelessly he piped:

> *"There is a tavern in the town . . . in the town . . .*
> *And there my true love sits him down . . . sits him*
> *down . . ."*

"Leave her be," Papa called from the ladder. "She's a big girl now."

"Danged if I know who she takes after," Harry said. "It sure ain't her mother. Louisa's the finest-looking woman in the county. No, nor the McAlisters either. She don't take after nobody that I can see."

"I guess I'm an original." Jen grinned.

"I'll say you are. Fresh, too. Hear that, Jamie? Young rascal says she's an original."

"I won't argue with that, Harry."

Jen buttoned her coat and pulled on her mittens. "I'm going to walk on home now. Are you ready to leave, Ella?"

"She's free." Papa backed carefully down the ladder. He scooped out a handful of candy from a glass jar on the counter and tumbled the peppermints into a paper sack. "You can take these along to Gram."

Jen touched his sleeve. "Will you be home for supper?"

"I'll try not to be late," he said. "But tell your mother not to wait."

"That awful old man," Ella said as she and Jen left the store. "He was in three times today checking on those cigars, just waiting for the rest to be sold so that he could grab the last one for nothing."

"Mr. Shomers isn't so bad," Jen told her. "Just talky and lonesome since his wife died. It's only a game he likes to play with Papa."

"A game James always loses!" Ella tucked her arm through Jen's as they hurried along the Brick Block in a rising wind. It had stopped snowing; overhead the first faint evening stars skated across a pale green winter sky. "Now tell me what you and that nice-looking boy were discussing."

"Davey? He wanted to know how I was going to decorate my lunch box for the Valentine Social so he could bid on it."

"I hope you told him!"

"No, it's against the rules. But I wanted to. Doing the right thing is hard sometimes, isn't it?" Jen asked. "At least for me it is. Now Luke was born good. He's never given Mama five minutes' trouble in his whole life. But I have to work at it, the way I work at sums."

"Being good is more than just staying out of trouble," Ella said. "It means caring about people, being considerate and kind. Like your father, for instance. That man has the patience of a saint. I've watched him all day being pleasant to customers, going out of his way to be helpful and obliging, listening to them go on about their aches and pains and pigs and politics . . . Now Lukas isn't like that. I honestly don't know what to make of him. I've been here three weeks and he's hardly spoken to me."

"I'm sure he admires you, Ella. We all do."

"Then why do I have the feeling he's making fun of me? And why is he so unsociable? Is it something I've done?"

"It isn't you," Jen said. "I think Luke's kind of bashful. And he likes to be alone. He reads a lot and writes things."

"What kind of things?"

"I don't know. He never lets me see."

They had turned down the River Road. Jen stopped abruptly. "Ella, *look!*" Across the river the sun was melting down along the distant bank; trees stood black and delicate against broad bands of shaded reds. From her window at home she had often tried to paint that scene, but she could never manage to capture the feelings it aroused. The vivid colors splashed along the horizon touched her in some thrilling way. Even when she was a child she had felt as if the seasons and weather flowed right through her . . . clouds and wind and snow and sunshine.

"It's so *real* here." Ella walked ahead with rapid energetic strides. "I'd forgotten that. It wasn't like that at all in Pittsburgh. The city was gray and noisy and dirty, but I did love the shops and theaters and restaurants, and the gas lamps coming on at night, and always having someplace else to go."

"You were happy there, weren't you?"

"I didn't have a worry in the world," Ella said, "and that's a kind of happiness. I should have been content. Leland was good to me. All he wanted was for me to dress up and make life pleasant for him when he was at home."

"I'm sure that was easy for *you* to do."

"I wanted to please him. He was a coal merchant, Jen . . . He'd always worked so hard. His hands were still cracked and lined with soot from all the labor of those years before. He liked nice things . . . He liked to run those big hard hands over the velvet furniture." She said, "It was wrong of me to feel that something was missing."

Jen said shyly, "If you had had children . . ."

"Leland wasn't interested in that. His own were grown and scattered before we met." Ella squeezed Jen's arm against her own. "But that's all behind me now. I guess you're stuck with me for a while."

"You can stay with us forever!"

"Only as long as I can be useful. Your mother spoils me so at home . . . that's why I want to help out at the store."

Jen had been a child when Ella left. Now she was certain they could be as close as sisters. "I'm so happy to have you back."

"Not Lukas!" Ella's laugh rang out in the crackling air. "Not Buttercup!"

8

Stays

Jen had been to the storeroom at McAlister's and sorted through piles of discarded boxes before she found exactly what she needed. Now, with all her equipment scattered on the dining room table, she was hard at work. Mama sat nearby, satiny flowers and tendrils of vines blossoming on the pillowslip she was embroidering. Close to the base burner Rock ran in his sleep. Jen thought Rock was a terrible name for a dog, but Charles insisted it was the happiest, snappiest one in the world, and Rock was his pet. His watchdog, he called it, even though the poor animal was so cross-eyed it would have been difficult for it to distinguish a bush from a burglar, and it was completely terrified of Puss.

Across from Jen, Maybelle sat watching, her small triangular face propped in her hands. "What if nobody bids on it?"

"I think somebody will."

Jen was pleased at how well it was going. She had transformed an oval hatbox into a sophisticated Gibson Girl with shining blue taffeta eyes, a red velvet mouth, and a shimmering pile of flossy golden hair. It looked, she thought, a little like Ella. Quickly she trimmed a hat to sit on top, with yards of tulle and odds and ends of bright ribbon. "I think Miss Phair would swoon with envy if she saw this."

"Do you have to be partners with whoever bids on it?"

"Yes, for the Social and the sleigh ride after."

"What if you don't like him?"

"There is only one male in the eighth grade that I entirely loathe."

"Who's that?"

"Old Rotten Roth."

"You mean Willard? That nice polite young man?" Mama looked up from her sewing in surprise. "What's the matter with him?"

"Lately he's been talking to us all in French . . . *his* version of it. Everything is *trez chick* instead of *très chic* and *say marvellouse* instead of *c'est merveilleuse*." Jen laughed and picked up the pheasant feathers Charles had offered from his treasure box. Somehow she'd work them in, in order not to hurt his feelings. He'd also offered a sling shot and the sinister skull of a skunk, but she had told him the feathers were the very thing she needed. And they did look pretty, woven in among the ribbons and tulle. "There. What do you think?" she asked her sister.

Maybelle shrugged. "I wouldn't waste my money bidding on it."

"Your face is green, little one."

"What does that mean?"

"That you are passionately jealous."

Mama murmured, "Stop teasing the child."

"She won't admit my creation is absolutely gorgeous."

"Keep in mind," Mama said, "that pride goeth before a fall."

From the parlor came the halting tones of the old rose-wood piano as Ella struggled to coax a tune from the chipped, yellowed keys.

> "Hello, ma baby . . . hello, ma honey . . . hello, ma ragtime gal.
> Send me a kiss by wire, tell me your heart's on fire."

Moments later the lid banged shut and Ella came out into the dining room, rubbing her hands together. "It's freezing in there!" She looked over Jen's shoulder. "Why, that's wonderful! You do have an artistic knack. Now tell me what you're going to wear to this gala affair."

"Her everyday is good enough," Mama said. "I won't have her catching her death in some flimsy rigamarole."

Jen made a despairing face. "My everyday is plain grotesque."

"I have something nice you could borrow," Ella told her. "May I lend her a dress, Louisa?"

Mama hesitated. "If you think it would be appropriate. I respect your good taste."

Upstairs, in Luke's old room with the bird's-eye maple bed and serviceable rag rug on the floor, Ella lit a lamp and groaned as she caught sight of herself in the mirror. "This awful black. If only mourning didn't have to look so sad and unbecoming."

Jen said, "It doesn't . . . not on you."

Ella sighed. "I feel as if I'm in the middle of a perpetual eclipse. Leland would hate seeing me looking like such a frump on his account." She opened the door to the closet. "Look at all these pretty things here waiting to kick up their heels." She ran her hands through the dresses, picked one out, looked at it critically, and handed it to Jen. "How about this one?"

It was a cherry-colored merino, smartly cut with simple lines.

"It's lovely. But will it fit?"

"Try it on."

Jen tripped over her petticoats in her hurry to get out of her clothes. The dress slid smoothly over her shoulders and down to the waist where it stuck fast. "I knew it wouldn't," she moaned. "I'll never have a shape like yours."

"We'll see about that." Ella opened a drawer and took out a pale pink undergarment stiffened with whalebone. "See if these will help."

"Stays?" Jen touched them gently. "Mama won't approve."

"She's not going to see them." Ella helped secure the corset in place, then began tugging at the laces at the back. "Hold your breath!"

"I'm choking!"

"That's good . . . !"

"Ella . . . I can't . . . breathe!"

"Fine. Now the dress is sure to fit." This time the red wool swirled over Jen's head, curved over her bodice, nipped in neatly at the waist, and dropped to her ankles in long graceful folds.

Ella was beaming. "That color is perfect with your hair."

"I love it! I love you! I'm going to run downstairs and show Mama."

"Better not. It isn't what I'd call a modest fit. Now I think it looks wonderful," Ella said, "but leave your mother to me."

Jen stared into the mirror. "If only I could borrow your face to go with it."

"What a thing to say! What's the matter with your own?"

"I'm not pretty. I'll never be pretty."

Ella looked at Jen for a long moment. "No, I don't think you will." She cupped the girl's chin in her hand, appraising her. "But your face is strong and interesting and alive. My looks will be gone in a minute . . . yours will last a lifetime, I'm sure of it. And someday you'll be beautiful, I promise you."

Nobody, not even Gram, had ever said anything like that before. Jen threw her arms around Ella, smelling her delicious rose-geranium fragrance. "Thank you! You're so good to me! What would I do without you?"

Ella laughed, hugging her back. "Better relax, honey . . . you're turning a bit blue. Here, let me loosen those stays. And Jen . . . this is our little secret . . . but they're yours to keep."

9

The Box Social

Jen glanced around the crowded cloakroom. There was no sign yet of Davey Sawyer. The usual nonsense was going on, boys snatching away scarves and mittens and excited girls, shining-eyed and trembling with nervous giggles, giving chase. Willard Roth wriggled by, giving her a painful poke in the ribs. "Don't forget, I'll be eating supper with you later on."

She inhaled the familiar smell of mothballs. "You don't know which lunch is mine!"

"Oh, don't I?" He had slanted reddish-brown eyes, and a narrow foxy face rusted all over with freckles. "Remember, Jen . . . where there's a Willard, there's a way."

Ignoring him, she bent to take off her overshoes, feeling the unaccustomed pinch of the stays. A sweet voice said, "That's a beautiful dress." It was Juanita Flatt, a slow, plump girl wearing her shapeless everyday plaid, but tonight she had a string of carved jet beads around her throat.

"Thanks, Juan. And that's a very pretty necklace."

They smiled at each other. Jen wished that Mary Frances Howard could be there to share the excitement, but her friend had been absent from school for a week with a sore throat and swollen glands.

Jen took a long shaky breath. She had been in charge of decorations and had stayed late after school to pin up lacy valentines, cupids, and crisscrossed red and white paper streamers. Tonight the classroom looked unfamiliar and romantic: scarred desktops and inkwells, dingy blackboards, maps, and wall charts indistinct among a sentimental landscape of hearts and flowers.

Across the room Davey was talking to Jessamine Doyle. The doctor's daughter had round pink cheeks, a tiny pink nose, and an enormous pink satin bow attached to the long blond ringlets hanging down her back. Her hair looked like the kind of unrealistic stuff that came attached to expensive imported dolls. Mary Frances said it was lightened with hydrogen peroxide from Dr. Doyle's medical supplies.

Jen wished Davey would look her way. They had been friends ever since he had moved into the village in September to live with his uncle, Asa Gentle. Because he was such a good student, his parents had decided that he should continue his education instead of working on the family farm; it was a sacrifice for them, and Davey worked hard to do well at his lessons. At first he and Jen had been seated side by side in class, but she had a habit of making him laugh out loud, and Miss Barrett had moved Jen to the very back row. The teacher was helping the boy prepare for the Regents examinations that he had to pass to enter high school.

"*Attention* . . . boys and girls, *if you please.*" Timidly Miss Barrett rapped on her desk. Awkward and self-conscious, she never seemed able to gain full control over her pupils. Nervously she touched the ginger poufs of hair at her temples and cleared her throat. "Since the sleigh will be arriving here at half-past six, I think we should start the bidding on the boxes now."

Her suggestion went unnoticed in the uproar. Jen felt sorry for Miss Barrett, for her tics and starts, her inability to take charge. Catching Davey's eye at last, Jen silently appealed to him to do something. Quickly he pushed his way through the crowd to stand beside the teacher. "Quiet, everyone! Miss Barrett thinks we ought to get things moving here!" He grinned. "If you're all as hungry as I am, then I'm sure you're ready to do as she says."

Grateful, Miss Barrett smiled at him. "A born leader," she often said of Davey, predicting that he'd enter politics one day.

"Boys, line up along the blackboards, please," she called out. "Girls, you may take your regular classroom seats."

"Say, Herby!" hissed Billy Arnold. "There's Juanita giving you the glad eye."

"Go 'wan . . ."

"She is! Imagine the size of the lunch she must have brought. You'd be a fool not to sit with her!"

Jen hoped that Juanita hadn't heard the remark. She hated it when the big, good-natured girl was teased about her size. As she slid into her desk against the wall Jessamine whispered across the aisle, "My stays are so tight that I think I'm going to faint."

"Don't you dare." Jessamine was a professional gasper and swooner. "I'll let you lie there and get trampled, I swear it," Jen told her.

"I'm aware that you have a heart of stone, Jen Mc-Alister."

"And you must have a granite head, considering the number of times you've landed on it," Jen said. "Even your brains must have calluses by now. And I can't imagine why your stays give you so much trouble when mine don't bother me in the least."

Jessamine stared in a sly, amused way. "I don't believe you're wearing them at all. Anyone can see that you don't have enough sticking out yet to have to hold in."

"All right, class . . . I believe we're ready to begin." Miss Barrett uncovered the heap of decorated boxes stacked on the desk in front of her. She lifted a heart-shaped one from the top. "Now who would like to start the bidding?"

"I will!" Danny Rowe's voice had a way of skidding up or down in the middle of a sentence. "Three cents!"

"Five!" someone else shouted.

"Six!"

"Ten!" There were no further bids. Miss Barrett turned over the box to find the owner's name on the bottom. "Then Daniel Rowe may claim the honor of sitting with Miss Annie Miller."

There was loud laughter and shouts of "Unfair!" Everyone knew that Dan had a crush on Annie. Then the auction continued with mingled cheers and jeers as each successful bidder discovered his supper partner. Herby Pole howled with dismay when he accidentally bid on Juanita's ample lunch and had to be boosted along to take a seat with her. As the pile slowly dwindled, Jessamine whispered, "Don't get your hopes up, Jen. Davey and I have arranged things between us."

"And what am I bid for this charming creation?" The teacher held up a shining pink box tied with glossy pink ribbons.

"Twenty-five cents!"

Jen was startled to discover it was Davey who had spoken. His cheeks were flushed, his fists clenched with concentration. None of the other boxes had gone for more than fifteen cents.

"We have an eager and magnanimous bidder," said Miss Barrett. "Would anyone care to raise that amount?"

Only a few boys were left standing. Willard, lounging casually against the blackboard with his hands in his pockets, said, "Nope. He's welcome to it."

"Then David Sawyer may have the pleasure of eating supper with . . ." All thumbs, Miss Barrett turned the box over and read out the name, "Jessamine Doyle."

"It may be bad cooking, but it sure is good looking," Herby sang out, as Davey came slowly down the aisle among hoots and whistles to take his place beside the triumphant girl. Across the aisle Jen sat in misery as the few remaining boxes were auctioned. Hers was the last.

The teacher's voice had almost given out. "Now what am I offered for this original Gibson Girl?"

"Five cents!" Willard spoke up. "Take it or leave it."

"Since you're our last bidder, I suppose I'll have to take it," Miss Barrett said. "But you have a bargain, Willard. You may go and sit with . . . Jennette McAlister."

Willard bounded happily down the aisle and squeezed in next to Jen, pinning her up against the wall.

"Who told you?"

"The fickle finger of fate arranged it all." Willard opened the lunch and rummaged busily inside. "Here, want a pickle?"

Jen tried to avoid any contact with his active knees and lethal elbows. "Somehow you found out . . . you *knew*."

Willard took a large juicy bite of chicken. "Say, did you pack any salt?"

"Was it Charles? Was it Maybelle?" Then Jen guessed the truth. "It was my sister who told you, wasn't it?

"Why can't you just relax and enjoy yourself?" Willard chewed noisily with his mouth open. "Come on, dig in! *Bone appeteet!*"

Jen ignored him when he asked if she had read about a terrible tidal wave in India that had swept thousands of Hindus into the sea. She wished he had been one of them. After looking forward to the Box Social for weeks, she couldn't wait for it to end.

There was a scramble in the cloakroom later as everyone shoved and jostled to find coats and overshoes. Behind her, Jen heard Davey whisper, "Sorry I made such a stupid mistake. Jess told me that the pink one was yours." Playfully he tugged at her scarf. "So let's have a good time anyway."

"Yes, let's." All the anticipation she had felt earlier bubbled up again.

10
The Sleigh Ride

The big sleigh waited outside the schoolhouse, Mr. Diebold hunched on the seat in his thick coat, smoking a pipe and muttering to the patient team. There was a fifteen-minute delay as the class waited for the chaperone to appear; then Reverend Williams's son puffed breathlessly across the yard with the news that his father had been called away on an emergency.

"But I can't take on the responsibility for such a large group alone," said Miss Barrett. There were shouts of protest, groans of disappointment.

"It's only for an hour," Davey told her. "The weather's clear and Mr. Diebold's an experienced driver."

Students crowded around the teacher, pleading with her to let them go. Wavering, she glanced at Davey. "You don't think there'll be any trouble?"

"I'm sure there won't be."

"All right," she decided. "Hop on, then!"

There was a rush as everyone piled on the sleigh, tumbling for places. Jen was grabbed around the waist and thrown face down into the cold, clean hay. Willard jumped up beside her and threw a musty blanket around her shoulders.

"Here, Davey!" Jessamine called out. "I've saved this nice warm robe for the two of us!"

Mr. Diebold clucked his teeth at the horses. Slowly the heavy sled glided out of the school yard, lanterns bobbing, catcalls and whistles rising shrilly in the frigid air. There was the creak of runners on the icy road, the hard, sweet clash of bells as they passed through the quiet village and on into the open country beyond. Here moonlight lay frozen white across the drifted fields. Jen, breathing deeply, leaned back and found herself braced against another body. Without turning she knew it was Davey. In spite of their bulky coats and the sliding motion of the sleigh, they stayed shoulder to shoulder, spine against spine, in a strange, blissful backwards embrace. All the warmth of Jen's feelings was focused where they touched, and the happy emotion she felt seemed the most intense and mysterious she had ever experienced. Laughter and voices surrounded them, but both were silent, conscious only of each other in the brimming beauty of the winter night.

For a time lazy flakes spiraled downward. Then, with a sudden rising of the wind, snow fell thicker, faster, the sky unbundling flapping blankets of white that soon blotted farmhouses, barns, and stooped silver orchards from sight.

"Perhaps we should be getting back." Miss Barrett, on her perch beside the driver, was uneasy, and Mr. Diebold, mumbling that he didn't like the look of things himself, watched for a place to turn around.

Resigned, the boys and girls burrowed deeper into the thick hay. Annie Miller, in a clear soprano, sang:

"Down by the old mill stream . . .
Where I first met you . . .
With your eyes so blue . . .
Dressed in gingham, too."

Davey Sawyer's deep voice joined in.

"It was there I knew . . .
That you loved me true."

"Jen," Willard said. "Take a look over here."

She turned. Willard gripped her by the arms and pressed a moist, desperate kiss on her half-open mouth. Furiously she struck out at him as Jessamine laughed and said loudly, "Of all people! Jen McAlister spooning!" It was then, as Mr. Diebold tried to make a turn, that the sleigh struck some buried object; in one confused moment bodies were bumping and falling, voices shouting and calling, the horses snorting and whinnying in alarm as the vehicle overturned.

Disoriented, Jen floundered out of a drift, saw dark shapes plunging around her in the swirling gusts.

"Somebody help me!" Jessamine Doyle, sprawled in the ditch, was holding her ankle and crying. Jen half dragged and half carried her toward a group huddled nearby.

"Where's Davey?" she asked, but the hysterical girl only sobbed louder.

"Is everyone all right?" Miss Barrett stumbled along the road, her voice shrill with panic, while the driver tried to soothe the frightened team. "Is everyone accounted for?"

Herby Pole, holding a lantern, peered under the up-turned runners. "There's a leg sticking out!"

"Get me out of here!" came a muffled voice, and several students hurried to pull Billy Arnold free. Jen searched from group to group, then ran back to the teacher. "I can't find Davey. Maybe he's trapped underneath!"

Boys surrounded the sled, arguing how to get it back on the road. To Jen their movements seemed clumsy and slow. She waded down to join them, straining as hard as she could with the rest.

"*Heave . . . heave . . .*"

"Come on," she pleaded. "*Hurry . . . hurry!*" The heavy vehicle rocked back and forth until, with one final groaning effort, they succeeded in turning it right side up. By the light of the lantern Jen saw Davey lying on his back in the ditch, covered with loose straw and snow, his legs twisted under him.

"David?" Miss Barrett knelt, brushing frozen particles out of his hair. "Can you tell us where you're hurt?"

His eyes were half-open and eerily unfocused, his breathing quick and shallow.

"He don't look so good to me," Mr. Diebold muttered. "We'd better get him to the doc real quick."

"Please, boys . . . lift him gently." Miss Barrett watched anxiously as Davey was placed on the sleigh. Frightened, Jen jumped up beside him, covered him quickly with a blanket, and wiped the blood from his mouth with her mitten.

Jessamine, her hat blown away, her long curls streaming in the wind, cried all the way back to town.

11

Waiting for the Crisis

February 25, 1900

Dear Davey,
I am so sorry about your misfortune, so sorry that you were
hurt

Jen stopped and looked critically at her strong slanted back-hand. Miss Barrett gave her poor marks in penmanship, and Mama said she was just being stubborn in not sloping her letters gracefully in the other direction. "There's a right and a wrong way of doing things."

"And there's Jen's way." Only Gram understood that the letters had a mind of their own. She picked up her pen again, dipped it in ink.

I would like to come and visit you, but your aunt says you must
be kept quiet and allowed to rest and so I guess I'll have to
wait but

But what? Jen groaned and fiercely crumpled up the paper. The words looked so cold and formal on the page. Why didn't she come right out and tell him how she missed seeing him in school, how worried she was about him? Ever since his parents had decided he should stay in the village instead of going home to recuperate she had known his condition must be serious. Not that his aunt had given out much information. Right after the accident Mama had baked a cake and gone to see what she could do, but Mrs. Gentle, an odd, suspicious little woman, hadn't even asked her into the house. The boy had broken a leg and some ribs, she said, and there was a danger of pneumonia, but no thank you, she didn't need help, and she and Mr. Gentle never ate sweets. So Mama had come home with her cake untasted and her kind offer rejected.

At school Jessamine, limping dramatically and carrying a crutch, told everyone that Dr. Doyle had promised that she could go and see Davey as soon as he was feeling better. It made Jen wildly jealous to think of it. The trouble was, he wasn't out of danger. Twice she had stopped by the Gentles' and knocked, but the blacksmith's wife, peeping out from behind the lace curtains, had refused to answer the door. Soon Jessamine reported that Davey had pneumonia and that her father was waiting for the crisis. At home and in church Jen prayed harder than usual, but in some sharp corner of her mind she questioned why good people often suffered worse afflictions than really disgraceful folks. The Claffins, for instance. Shiftless Mr. Claffin loafed, shrill Mrs. Claffin cussed, and their impudent girls reared lusty babies without any husbands in sight, and yet they were skipped over every time. Life wasn't fair!

"The Lord has His reasons," was Mama's explanation of any calamity. Jen was baffled as to what those reasons might be. Pneumonia was a deadly killer, and until the crisis was reached all anyone could do was pray. "Please

God, I'll give up anything, even my dearest possessions, if only You'll make him well again," she bargained, head bent, hands tightly clasped. But what, she wondered, could one offer in exchange? Paints and brushes, her prized arrowheads, a favorite dog-eared edition of *David Copperfield*? She'd give them all willingly if Davey would recover. "Don't let him die!"

The one thing that made her laugh during this troubled time was her father's tale of Rheba Watson and her Raiders. Papa came home almost every evening now as soon as he closed McAlister's, and Jen thought it must be Ella's good influence. As she bent over her homework in the dining room, she would hear distant singing on the River Road, and listen as Luke's baritone, Ella's light soprano, and her father's beautiful tenor blended in:

> *"I dream of Jeannie with the light brown hair,*
> *Borne like a zephyr on the summer air."*

or

> *"Beautiful dreamer, wake unto me,*
> *Starlight and dewdrops are waiting for thee."*

or some of the other Stephen Foster melodies that Papa loved so much, the voices getting closer and closer until the three of them arrived, flushed from the cold and stamping the snow from their boots. There would be strong pleasure in Mama's voice as she called out, "Just in time! Supper's ready!"

One night they came in so talkative and high-spirited that Gram, hearing the commotion, bobbed eagerly down the stairs to find out what was going on.

"James will tell you all about it," Ella laughed, but Mama, carrying the china soup tureen from the range, said, "First we'll say grace."

Jen felt a circular comfort these nights as they all sat down together, Rock's tail banging hopefully beneath the kitchen table and winter huddled outside the house, rattling at the windows, unable to get in.

"What happened?" Charles asked his father, as soon as the *amens* were spoken.

"It was about four o'clock this afternoon," Papa began, "when I decided to nip on over to Dewey's . . . to make a delivery. Now maybe you know it and maybe you don't, but Dewey is a bit lax in taking down his Christmas decorations, and we were joshing him about it."

As a matter of fact, Jen did know. She had peeked in often enough to have noticed that, months after the holiday, holly and ivy and red paper bells still festooned the walls of the tavern.

"So there we were, Tom O'Connell (who sends along his best regards to you, Louisa), Eustace Bean and myself, and this slick drummer fellow from New York City, with a sample case full of shoes to peddle, having a friendly glass, when all of a sudden we heard this queer hubbub out on the street. All of a sudden the front window exploded — smashed to smithereens before our very eyes, and the front door blew open and there she stood, six feet tall and majestically outraged . . . urging her Raiders to come in and bust up the joint."

"Rheba Watson!" Jen laughed.

"Everyone eat before supper gets cold," Mama said, ladling steaming oxtail soup, but no one but Gram paid any attention.

"In she came," Papa went on, "with four or five of her evangelical cronies, waving rolling pins and umbrellas and pokers, smashing mirrors, knocking the glasses off the bar, spearing down the Christmas trimmings, all of them screeching and carrying on like banshees. Dewey pulled his apron up over his head," (here Papa hid behind his napkin with only his bright eyes showing) "and it was every man for himself — bellies and behinds bumping as everyone scattered. Except the four of us who just sat there dumbfounded. That poor drummer fellow was scared witless, for along came Rheba and gave his sample case one mighty kick" (Papa's knee jerked under the table and Rock flew out and skidded off into the living room), "and there was the most democratic dance of footgear you ever saw in your life — hobnailed boots and evening pumps and bitty baby shoes skipping and jigging away in all directions. 'I am an instrument of the Lord,' Rheba hollered, and slashed out with her umbrella and sent our glasses flying. Then she rounded up her gang and they sashayed out of there, as pleased as punch with themselves." Papa mopped his brow theatrically with his napkin. " 'Who in hell was that?' the salesman asked me. 'That pious steeple of a woman,' I told him, 'is Mrs. Rheba Watson, and she has it in for alcohol and sin,' and I told him how she'd been rampaging loose for over a year now, ever since the holy fits came over her."

Everyone laughed except Mama, who seemed troubled. She was fond of Mrs. Watson and sympathized with her. Maybe, Jen thought, Mama would have liked to help tear up the tavern.

Papa wasn't finished yet. " 'It's my opinion dangerous instruments like that ought to be locked up in a safe place,' the drummer told us. None of us much liked his tone. Eustace tried to explain that under ordinary circumstances Rheba was a fine woman, and baked the most wonderful rhubarb custard pies for church socials, and looked out for orphans and fallen women whenever she could find any, but we couldn't convince him that *we* weren't as crazy as she was for putting up with it."

In school the next day Jen learned from Jessamine that Davey had survived the crisis after all. Deeply relieved, she decided to pass along the tale of Rheba Watson and her Raiders in a series of cartoons to cheer up his sickbed and make him laugh. Yet even though it was an amusing story, part of her envied "that pious steeple of a woman" for being the first female courageous enough to invade the sanctuary of the all-male saloon.

12

A Birthday Surprise

On the tenth of March Jen woke with a feeling of excitement. It was her fourteenth birthday. *Fourteen!* Out of the whole year she owned this one day completely, could shine with importance, receive gifts, share cake and congratulations. She could never understand why older women grimaced over such events as if they were a nuisance. Not Gram; she fiercely celebrated every one, and Jen hoped to be just like her.

Maybelle woke, as she usually did, with a frown on her face.

"It's my birthday," Jen reminded her.

"So?"

"That makes me special."

"You're already special." Maybelle scowled harder. "You get to do everything first."

"Like what?"

"Like being fourteen."

After the younger girl had gone downstairs Jen allowed herself an extra few minutes in bed, but it was hard to enjoy it. Yet she thought she understood how Maybelle must feel. Not only were clothes passed along to be pinned up and adjusted, but sometimes it must seem as if even her experiences were secondhand.

There was a knock at the door. Charles burst in and hopped, skipped, and jumped over to the bed. Rock pranced behind him, wagging his stump of a tail, and stumbled into the wastebasket. "I have something for you." Charles thrust something into her hand, a cold, damp knob with dirt sticking to it.

"What is it?"

"Don't you know? It's a truffle!"

"A truffle?"

"Rock dug it up. You remember what Maybelle said, how you find them underground and how good they taste and how much they cost?"

"I remember."

"Are you going to eat it now?"

The thing felt horrible. "I'll save it for later, Charles. But thank you . . . a truffle . . . imagine that!"

"That isn't all."

She had hoped that it was.

"This is for you, too. I found it down by the lake."

It was an arrowhead, chipped from a lustrous piece of smooth green stone. Indian artifacts lay scattered throughout the area but were becoming harder and harder to find. Jen had her own collection, assembled over many years, but this was a rarity, a perfect specimen. She hugged him. "Oh, Charles . . . it really is a beauty. Thank you for such a wonderful present!"

He hopped, skipped, and jumped again; he was practicing for the Fourth of July competitions, months away. "I was joking about the truffle. It's just an old butternut that a squirrel buried. You don't really have to eat it." Both of them laughed, delighted with his joke.

"Will you be stopping in at the store today?" Papa asked at breakfast. He looked as if he knew a secret.

"Why? Do you want me to?" Jen asked.

"There is an errand I'd like you to do for me after school." He glanced at Mama and she nodded, smiling faintly, as if something had been approved between the two of them. Jen wondered what it was as she ate; eggs and warm muffins looked the same but tasted so much better served this morning on a Limoges china plate.

Puss followed her as she went upstairs with her grandmother's coffee.

"Well, here's the birthday girl at last! Thought you'd forgotten all about me."

"Have I ever forgotten you?"

"Well, on a special day like this . . ."

Gram's little room was cluttered with all sorts of bric-a-brac: old newspapers, letters and photographs, a heap of afghan she was knitting, yards of crocheted lace to be sewed onto pillow cases, and piles and piles of books. Like Papa, she loved to read.

She held out a package to Jen. "Now hurry up and open this before you leave for school." Inside was a square of white cotton, with a yellow sun on it, beaming brilliant spokes of orange.

"You're making me a quilt?"

"Yes, for your hope chest. This is the first piece, and when I'm finished with the others you can help me stitch them together."

"It's beautiful! I can't wait to see it!"

Puss lingered hopefully by the door. "Look at that stuck-up thing just waiting for my chair." Gram waved her hands. "Shoo, cat! Scat!"

"I have to go." Jen kissed her grandmother and gave her an extra hug. "It's going to be a wonderful quilt."

"Happy Birthday!"

A soft March day, clouds flapping briskly overhead, the pleasant *plip plip plip* of melting snow. People were out of doors early, chatting on street corners, eager to stretch and ease the winter-cramped, sociable sides of themselves. Jen, on her way to school, smelled fresh lumber in the air and heard hammers knocking against wood as workmen repaired the livery stable. She caught a rainbow glimpse of spring bonnets in Miss Phair's and couldn't resist stopping for a look. Then she ran the last long block for fear she would be late.

Mary Frances was waiting for her. She was a thin, plain girl with patches of eczema on her hands and neck, but when she smiled her face shone as if a lamp had been turned on inside. "I thought you'd never get here! Quick, open this! I can't wait for you to see it!"

It was an autograph album with red plush covers, and rose-colored pages.

"I'll keep it forever," Jen told her as they hurried to class. "And I want you to be the first to sign."

During the morning the album was passed secretively back and forth along the aisles, and at recess Jen read what her schoolmates had written. On the fly leaf Mary Frances expressed her sentiments in a flowing script.

> *True friendship is so sweet and rare,*
> *And this book shows how much I care.*

"Look at this . . ." With a laugh Jen showed her friend where Jessamine had scribbled:

> *When I am dying, and sigh and moan,*
> *I won't forget your heart of stone.*

and carelessly splotched ink all over the page. Juanita had laboriously penned:

> *You are a pal so fine and true.*
> *I wish I were as thin as you.*

And Willard Roth brilliantly invented:

> *Roses are red, violets are blue,*
> *Sugar is sweet, but oh! not you.*
> *Yet no matter what you say or do,*
> *I could never be untrue.*
> *(Yr's 'til Niagara Falls)*

"Even his verse smells of mothballs," Mary Frances said, and went into fits of giggles.

During lunch hour the teacher wrote neatly in the album with letters that sailed like tall ships to the east:

BE CAREFUL

Be careful of your
manners, for they
indicate your
breeding.
Be careful of your
thoughts, for they
form your life.
Be careful of your
actions, for they
reveal your
character.
Be careful of your
associates, as you
are judged by the
company you keep.

"Thank you, Miss Barrett." Jen was polite but she thought that taking such a cautious approach to life would be very uninteresting. From time to time during the afternoon she looked toward Davey's empty seat and wondered what he would have written if he had been there.

After school, as she cut across the school yard on her

way to McAlister's, a voice called after her, "Wait for me!"

It was Maybelle, running to catch up, and breathlessly complaining, "I wish I could be fourteen."

Jen hoped her sister wasn't going to horn in on her father's birthday plans. "You will be someday."

"It won't be the same. Mama favors Luke and Ella, and you're Gram's favorite, and everyone fusses over Charles, but nobody cares about me. Just because I'm so ugly."

"You're not ugly." Jen glanced at Maybelle, noticing the delicacy of the small features, the rich sheen of copper in the filmy brown hair, the hazel eyes, set far apart, as deep and worried as Mama's. "You have a very pretty face," she said, "especially when you smile. I think you should try to do it more often."

"I do try. But even when I try harder to be better than everybody else, it doesn't make any difference."

"That's silly. We're all proud of you. Look how smart you are! Aren't you the best speller in your class?"

"I'm the best with figures, too," Maybelle bragged. "One of these days I'm going to get my hands on Papa's book-keeping records and then I'll settle those accounts."

"You mustn't try *too* hard," Jen told her. "Like marking down sins for instance. I think you're wasting your time."

"All right." Maybelle was meek. "Anyway, you didn't have *that* many." She took Jen's hand and held it. "I want to be just like you when I grow up."

It touched and surprised Jen to think that her sister might look up to her the way she did to Ella, and Ella to Mama. Being older was a big responsibility. She would

have to be more attentive and patient with the little wor-
rywart walking beside her. It wouldn't be easy, but starting
today she would make an effort.

Papa had left Luke in charge and was waiting outside
of the store, dressed in his smart Prince Albert coat and
his best blue and black striped shirt with the celluloid
collar and cuffs. "Ready, Jen?"

"Where are we going?"

"Come along, you'll see."

"Can't I go too?" Maybelle whined.

"If it's all right with your sister," Papa said and Jen,
remembering her good intentions, nodded graciously. Her
father offered each girl an arm and then escorted them
down the street. Spring was definitely in the air; Mr. Mock
was showing the latest thing in dining-room suites to a
newlywed couple, and in the hardware store a clerk was
pulling out fresh rolls of wallpaper for a customer's inspection.

A strange thing happened. As they stood outside Miss
Phair's Millinery Establishment, with sunlight sparkling
through the plate-glass windows, Jen was back inside her
winter dream, gazing at all the lovely bonnets on display.
Then Papa lifted the latch on the door and stood aside for
the girls to pass. "Ladies? Shall we go inside?"

A bell tinkled softly. The air was faintly perfumed. Ivy
spilled from a wicker planter in the corner. There was an
Oriental carpet on the floor, and fragile chairs, and hats
everywhere, hats as light and airy as meringues floating
on tall, honey-colored wooden spindles.

The proprietress bustled out from behind a blue velvet curtain at the back. "Well, Jamie, what can I do for you today?"

Papa drew Jen forward by the hand. "Do you think you can find something special enough for a young lady on her fourteenth birthday?"

"I should certainly hope so." Tiny Miss Phair toddled around Jen, taking baby steps and looking at her from all angles.

"What we would like," Papa said, gazing slowly around the shop, "is the most charming, the most elegant, the most spectacular hat in the place." He leaned against the wall and confidently folded his arms across his chest. "Go ahead, Jen. Try one on. Try them all on if you like."

How could she choose? Awkwardly Jen picked up the one nearest to her and set it squarely on her head.

"Oh, no, my dear!" Miss Phair rushed to make fussy adjustments, turning the bonnet this way and that, primping out the ribbons. She handed Jen a long-handled mirror so that she could catch the effect from the back. Twenty minutes later Jen still wasn't able to decide from among the clouds of tulle and swirls of satin, the flowers and fruit and billowing ostrich feathers.

"Don't you see anything you like?" Papa asked.

"I think I'm in love with them all."

"Then what we must do," he told the shopkeeper, "is try to match the girl with the hat. Now all of these are very lovely, but don't you have anything with a little more . . . *snap?*"

Jen thought Miss Phair would be offended, but instead her childish expression brightened. "I do have something that came in from New York this week. It is rather sophisticated for a young girl, but if you'd like to take a look . . ."

"Certainly we would." Papa was in no hurry at all. He was enjoying himself. Unlike most men, he was deeply interested in women's fashions.

Miss Phair disappeared into the back room and then emerged a few minutes later carrying a large oval box. Her little plump hands swooped in among the crushed tissue and brought out a hat: white, a flippant brim trimmed with bright bunches of crimson cherries, with matching ribbons to tie beneath the chin. Jen knew it at once, knew exactly the way to tilt it into place. Dazzled, the dark-eyed girl in the mirror asked, "Papa?" He was never wrong in such important matters.

For one long delicious moment they stared at each other. Then he bent and brushed her cheek with his thick black mustache in the old affectionate way. "That's your hat."

"Thank you." It was all that needed to be said. He hadn't even asked about the price.

"What about me?" Maybelle's eyes brimmed with envy as she sat with her fists curled tightly in her lap.

Nothing must spoil the pleasure of this day. Jen asked her father, "Do you think she could have one, too?"

He barely hesitated. "It *is* almost Easter bonnet time. All right, Maybelle . . . pick out any one you like."

"Which one, my dear?" prompted Miss Phair.

"*That* one." Triumphantly Maybelle pointed to the one that Jen was wearing. "I want one exactly like that."

Jen sucked in her breath.

Miss Phair was apologetic. "I'm sorry, child. That is one of a kind. But never mind, I'm sure we can find another quite as nice."

Fifteen minutes later when they left the shop, both carrying boxes, Jen saw that Maybelle's face was just as radiant as her own. Such a gift, such a birthday, such a remarkable father! She couldn't wait to show her grandmother the most beautiful hat in the world.

13

An Offer of Employment

"Don't move," Jen said. "I'm almost finished." She was working quickly in pastels, trying to catch the colored lights dancing in Ella's crinkled hair.

"I've always had trouble sitting still."

It hadn't been as easy as Jen expected. The warm skin tones, for instance. Ella looked as if she had been rubbed all over in warm sand, but catching that glow with soft chalk on paper was difficult. And the sparkle was missing from her expression today, as she posed with a red shawl thrown over her black dress. "Is something the matter?"

"I guess I'm just a little restless."

Or bored, Jen thought. Ella liked change and variety. Once she had run away to catch hold of excitement; how small and dull and quiet Aurora must seem after the crowds and activity of the city.

"And," Ella sighed, "I've been feeling guilty about your mother."

"Why?"

"She has a hard life, Jen."

"She does? Mama doesn't complain."

"I know. But think of the drudgery . . . the fixed routine."

Jen did think about it. Mama scheduled a different chore for every day of the week. On Mondays all the soiled clothing seethed and simmered in a big copper boiler on the stove, was scrubbed and rinsed, the white things dipped in bluing, everything starched and wrung out by hand. Then the loaded baskets were carried out into the yard where, in freezing weather, the lines creaked and swayed with stiffened shirts and frozen bedding and crackling undergarments. When Jen and Maybelle came home from school they carried the laundry back into the house where each piece was thawed, sprinkled, tightly rolled, and set aside for the next day.

Ella said, "In Pittsburgh I had an Irish girl named Rosie Flanagan who worked for me. What a foul mouth the dear girl had — she could cuss like a sailor — but she had the most delicate touch in the world with fine lingerie, all the tucks and ruching. Oh, the good times and the laughs we had together, and what wouldn't I give to see her again."

Nobody was as particular about the ironing as Mama. On Tuesdays, with flatirons kept hot on the stove, she pressed everything from the smallest handkerchief to the bulkiest bedsheet satin-smooth and put them away with the fresh smell of outdoors folded inside. Wednesdays, with her quick needle and worn silver thimble, she patched the torn clothing, secured dangling buttons, turned frayed shirt collars, darned stockings, and helped stitch the beautiful quilts that Gram designed; there was one displayed on each bed in her home. Thursdays and Fridays she attacked every corner of the house in two exhausting days of scrubbing, mopping, waxing, and polishing. "Louisa's floors are so clean you can eat off them," Gram used to brag when Jen was little and took things too literally, and one day was discovered doing just that.

"Now may I see?" Ella stretched and yawned.

"In a minute. I'm almost finished."

Jen loved the smell of Saturdays best, when the fragrance of fresh-baked bread and rolls filled the air. She enjoyed kneading the dough, spanking its plump spongy contours with floury hands while her mother made pies and cakes, muffins and doughnuts, and Maybelle washed the pots and pans. Sunday was supposed to be a day of rest, but Mama went to church services morning and evening and cooked a big midday meal in between. Yet most women did the same, spent a lifetime in hard physical labor, rearing children, with little time for fun. With a sudden shock Jen wondered if that was all that lay ahead for her. She detested housework; when would she find time to draw or paint with all those other tedious things to do?

"Leland would never let me lift a finger," Ella murmured, trying not to jiggle. "I don't know how Rosie managed it all."

Jen was tired of hearing about wonderful Rosie. And it wasn't surprising why Ella had been so fond of her. Yet it didn't seem fair that the immigrant girl had done all the work while Ella simply enjoyed herself. No wonder she was depressed. Her old carefree existence was over and it was obvious how much she missed it.

"I'm getting a crick in my neck," she complained.

"All right." Satisfied, Jen dusted off her hands. "Now you can have a look."

"Why, that's marvelous!" Ella was impressed and pleased. "You do have a knack for catching a likeness. Let's show it to your mother."

"No." Jen knew better. "If she knows I'm doing this she'll think up something practical for me to do."

How different the two of them were. Only when she was using her hands this way did Jen feel she was involved in something worthwhile and important. Yet Mama only saw it as frivolous, a waste of time. And was probably right, Jen thought, although something stubborn in her still wondered about that.

On their way home from Wednesday evening prayer meeting at St. John's, Luke and Jen bumped into Thomas O'Connell. He was pleased to see them and asked if they would step up to his office above Mock's Undertaking and Furniture Store. "Remember that talk we were supposed to have, Luke?"

"I've been pretty busy lately, Mr. O'Connell."

"Quite all right . . . let's take care of it now. I won't take much of your time."

Single file they walked up the dark crooked staircase. At the top the lawyer asked Jen for his key.

"I don't have it."

"Take a look in your coat pocket."

Marveling as always at his magic, she fished it out and handed it over. Inside, Mr. O'Connell lit a lamp and invited them to sit down. "Luke, how would you like to come and clerk for me?"

Luke didn't seem so surprised by the offer. Jen suspected that he had been dodging the question for weeks.

"I like you, son. I know that you have an excellent mind and I'd like to see you do something with it. Not that I'm implying that working in McAlister's doesn't take brains, of course it does. But it has occurred to me that you might be interested in doing something else with your life." He glanced around at the crowded bookshelves, the files scattered across his desk. "Frankly, I could use the help."

Jen liked the man. She admired his gaunt good looks, the dark wing of hair combed flat against his high white forehead. Her mother didn't approve of him because of his relationship with Bessie Trowbridge, who ran the boardinghouse behind the depot, but Jen knew he thought highly of Mama. She wondered if he might have courted her years ago.

Luke shifted in his chair, turning his cap around and around in his hands. "I don't know much about the law, sir."

"Then I'll tell you something. You would have to work very hard and the rewards, when there are any, are usually financial, seldom spiritual." A smile gleamed briefly on the man's pale face. "When a client sees his attorney on the street it hardly ignites a bright blaze of fellowship in his heart. Instead it reminds him of things that frighten or annoy him . . . death and taxes, for instance. And he's bound to feel wary of someone who knows the dark side of his moon . . . his avarice, guilt, thirst for revenge, lust for property, et cetera. And yet, in spite of this universal suspicion toward our maligned profession, some of us still manage to retain our pure regard for the law, that exasperating necessity that enables human beings to conduct their lives without clubbing each other into submission."

Jen enjoyed hearing Mr. O'Connell talk, even when he was sometimes difficult to understand. For the next few minutes the men discussed what Luke's duties would be, his salary, and his prospects once his training was completed.

Luke was polite. "It's an excellent offer . . . but my father might be disappointed if I left McAlister's. The store's been handed down to the sons in the family for generations."

"Son, there's nothing in the Ten Commandments about disrupting old family traditions. Besides, I've already spoken to your father . . . he is my oldest, dearest friend. Of course I wouldn't try to entice you here behind his back. For some reason he suspects you're not happy where you are. He has your best interests at heart, after all. He urged me to talk to you."

Yes, Papa would be fair, Jen was sure of it, no matter what he might want for himself. Not that Luke would give him credit for that.

"Then there's Mama," Luke said. "She's always had her heart set on me going into the Seminary someday. I think it might break her heart if I don't become a clergyman."

"This might surprise you — " Mr. O'Connell picked up his pen from the desk and Jen saw it disappear into thin air — "but I wouldn't worry about breaking her heart. Contrary to public opinion and popular songs, those maternal organs are *not* as fragile as china plates. When I was your age and somewhat disgracefully sowing my own wild oats, my dear mother's heart didn't chip, crack, or shatter once. But when I finally settled down into an honest profession, I will testify here and now that the poor woman expired of the most awful boredom."

Jen laughed. She knew he was joking but her brother looked uncomfortable. The lawyer got to his feet and shook hands with Luke. "Tell your parents that we've had this chat and take some time to think it over. The law isn't such a bad life. In fact, I consider it downright fascinating." While his hands were in his pockets, the missing pen had suddenly appeared behind his ear. "Remember, Luke . . . man's inhumanity to man has always challenged the keenest minds. And beneath the malice and the greed, you might be surprised at what you turn up. Certainly enough humor to keep your heart from freezing over." He smiled at Jen. "And now, young lady . . . if you'll just hand me back that key . . ."

"Mr. O'Connell, I don't . . ."

"In your overshoe, my dear."

14

A Family Argument

Good Friday was sullen and gloomy, but Easter Sunday was radiant with sunshine and warm enough for finery. Jen and Maybelle preened in their new bonnets while Ella scowled at her black hat in the pier glass in the hall. Gram never went near St. John's, and yet every so often Mama tried to change her mind. Everybody went to church, she said; even the Claffins straggled off to Mass at St. Bernard's once a week. "It just doesn't look right, Mrs. McAlister. You know how people talk."

It was the one prickly issue between the two older women. Gram said, "If I embarrass you, Louisa, then you can say I'm ill."

"But you're never sick."

"Yes, I am. Sick and tired of you fretting about my soul!"

Just before the family left the house, Jen ran upstairs to try some persuasion of her own. "It would be so much nicer if you'd come with us, Gram. I know you'd love the music and the flowers. Please . . . just this once?"

"I'm not a-going. Not now, not next week, not ever."

"But why not?"

"It wouldn't be right or honest, that's why not." Gram was working on the sunburst quilt and sucking on a peppermint. "The church is a house of peace . . . and love. There's no room in it for a tough old sinner like me."

Jen laughed at that idea. "You aren't a sinner."

"Oh, but I am. There's anger in me, stuck like a splinter of ice in my heart."

"Who are you angry with?"

"Why, God, of course. I'm mad at Him and don't tell me that's not sinful!"

"But you can't be mad at *God*. It's impossible . . . that would be unforgivable."

"Don't you think I know it? But that's the way it is."

Jen sat on the bed and stared at her grandmother. She was shocked and interested. "But why?"

"The Bible says that the Lord giveth and the Lord taketh away. But He went too far, He took too much. First my little sister when her nightgown caught fire, and I'll never forget the flames or her pitiful cries until the day I die. A helpless child, Jen . . . Why did she have to suffer so? Then both my parents taken with influenza. I was left with twin brothers to raise, the dearest lads that ever were, Edwin and Ernest. Both of them killed in that terrible war on the very same day at Antietam. *Enough*, I said. *Enough*. And I married Hiram and had my own sweet babes and suckled and cherished them and one by one He took them all away from me." Gram took off her spectacles and wiped her eyes with the back of her hand. "That's when I fought back. I was thirty-seven then, too old for child-bearing, but I gave birth to one more son and I swore I'd never let him go. Every time that boy got sick I'd hang on and holler, 'You can't have this one — he's mine!' And Jamie stayed."

She polished her glasses over and over with one of the cotton squares. "Then Hiram was taken, my lovely man. Why, Jen? All those precious lives, those bitter tears." Gram was weeping over her old buried griefs, her face hidden in her hands. Jen went to put her arms around her.

"Please don't cry. Mama says the Lord has His reasons."

"Oh, does He? Then I'd like to hear what they are."

"She says we have to have faith and trust in His wisdom."

"That may be all very well for Louisa, but it's not good enough for me. Maybe I love too hard . . . and I warn you, Jen . . . I see the very same fault in you . . . but I won't kneel and be thankful for pain or the cruel fact of death. It's life I care about, and life for me is here in this house and not in a church." She picked up her sewing again. "There. I've told you the awful truth, and that's the end of it. It's nothing for you to worry about, and I wish your mother would stop nagging me. When the time comes I'll take the matter up with the Lord myself, and He'd better have some answers for me, that's all I can say. Until then, let me be."

Later, in St. John's, Jen's eyes lifted to the gorgeous saints and apostles and innocent lambs strolling across the stained-glass windows. She was confused by what she had learned that morning. Beliefs that had been instilled in her since earliest childhood had been shaken. Gram challenged a rough God of Vengeance while Mama trusted a benign God of Love. Which one was right?

The thrilling crescendo of the organ, the waxen purity

of Easter lilies, sunlight flowing through gem-colored panes . . . wasn't the beauty glowing at the heart of the mystery an affirmation of her mother's point of view? It was certainly safer and more comforting to think so. Yet remembering what her grandmother had said, considering all the suffering in the world around her, for the first time Jen wondered.

Everyone was hungry for dinner, succulent glazed ham with all the trimmings. Jen noticed that her grandmother had recovered her good spirits and ate with her usual hearty appetite.

"By the way," Luke said, as Jen and Maybelle cleared away the dishes, "Mr. O'Connell said he'd be dropping by this afternoon. He's made me an offer, and I'm going to give him an answer today."

Mama was startled. "What kind of an offer?"

"He's asked me to clerk for him."

"Lukas, how wonderful!" Ella reached over to squeeze his hand. "And what an honor."

"An honor? To work for a man like that?" A fine white line tightened around Mama's lips.

"Ella's right," Papa said. "Our boy has been offered a rare opportunity."

"You don't seem surprised about it."

"Thomas asked me about this some time ago, dear. And I encouraged him to go ahead and speak to Luke."

"Well, then . . ." Mama looked at her oldest son defiantly. "What have you decided?"

"I'm going to do it."

"Just like that! Without a word of advice from anyone?"

"The boy *is* eighteen, now." Gram, who seldom inter-
fered, spoke up. "I suspect that's old enough to know his
own mind."

"I'm not really certain this is what I want to do with
the rest of my life," Luke said, "but I have to find out.
And I haven't been happy working at the store. I think
Papa knows that."

"If you intend to go into the law, then I suppose it is
your own affair," said his mother. "But with the likes of
Thomas O'Connell? I hope you don't expect my blessing!"

"It's because of Bessie Trowbridge, isn't it?"

"Little pitchers have big ears," Mama reminded Luke
sternly. "Maybelle and Charles, would you kindly leave
the table while we finish this conversation?"

"But surely, Louisa," Gram spoke up again, "you wouldn't
deprive the children of dessert?"

"Very well. We'll talk about this after we finish dinner,"
Mama decided.

Nobody spoke as the lemon meringue pie was served.
The only sounds were the forks scraping against the plates
and Rock whining softly at the back door wanting to be
let in. Coffee was poured in silence. Charles, eager to
escape, asked to be excused, then hopped, skipped, and
jumped out of the dining room. Maybelle, hairbows twitch-
ing, sat stubbornly in her place until Mama said, "Now
you run along, too." Tearful at missing out, the girl whispered spitefully, "It isn't fair that *you* get to stay!" on her
way past Jen's chair.

"All right, Mama . . ." Luke picked up the argument where it had been dropped. "It's because of Bessie you object . . . admit it!"

"Bessie Trowbridge is a generous, hardworking woman," Papa said, "and she's been very good to Thomas over the years, but that has nothing to do with whether you should clerk for him."

"It has everything to do with it as far as Mama is concerned."

"Have I ever said one word against that woman?" Mama's cheeks were flushed with indignation. "All I know is that a person is judged by the company he keeps, and I hate the idea of my boy being tarred by the same brush as that immoral man."

"That's ridiculous! He's a skilled professional, and that's all that matters!" Luke insisted.

"Louisa . . ." Papa spoke gently. "If our son can find a better future somewhere else, then what's the harm? The door is always open at the store if Luke wants to come back."

"I won't even be missed, now that Ella's there."

"Ella's a grand help, and I don't know what I'd do without her . . . but you certainly will be missed," Papa said.

"Mr. O'Connell thinks that Luke has an excellent mind." Jen hoped that things were smoothing over.

"Indeed." Mama set down her coffee cup and rubbed her temples. "Well, I can see that everyone here approves. Apparently I was the only one left in the dark."

"I knew that you'd be upset," Luke told her. "I wanted to make up my own mind before I told you."

"Well, you picked a fine time, I must say! I hope you're satisfied now that you've ruined Easter dinner."

"Nothing is ruined, yet." Ella appealed to Mama. "Lukas has made an important decision. So let's all be happy for him."

"I'll thank you to stay out of this," Mama said. "This is a family matter."

Jen had never heard her mother speak this way before. "But Ella *is* family!"

"No, I'm not . . . of course, I'm not." Quickly the young woman rose from the table. "I'm sorry. I had no right to interfere."

"Mama!" Luke threw down his napkin. "How could you hurt her that way?" His chair clattered as he got to his feet and followed Ella out of the room.

"Louisa . . ." Papa sighed. "Oh, Louisa . . ."

"If you'll excuse me . . ." Now Mama rose. "I feel a headache coming on."

"You go upstairs and lie down," Jen told her. "Maybelle and I will take care of the dishes." She could hardly believe what her mother had said. It was because she loved Luke so much that she had spoken those cruel words and Jen hoped her brother would find some way to reassure Ella that she was one of them and not an outsider.

15

A Reconciliation

Warner arrived early in May and stayed until June. She was an angular woman, always dressed soberly in gray, with a tight knob of steel-gray hair and a mouth grimly puckered from holding pins in it. Jen couldn't imagine a spring without Warner stitched firmly in the middle of it. Deftly she turned bolts of muslin into bedding, sewed shirts for the males and lingerie for the females, made up dress lengths into one summer and one winter garment each for the girls, and carefully picked apart, cut up, and converted old things into new ones. Jen didn't know if Warner was her first name or her last, whether she had ever been married, or if she liked the borrowed life she led, trying on one household after another every month of the year. She did know that Warner didn't care too much for young folk. Charles was too fidgety, Maybelle too particular, and Jen grew too fast to suit her. She had a calculating way of squinting at them, as if she'd like to shorten or lengthen them more to her liking. Yet Jen had always been fascinated by her austere face and bony frame, and she liked sketching Warner while she was at work.

"Why pick on me?" the seamstress snapped. "Ella's the beauty."

"I think you have character," Jen told her.

"Character." Warner sighed and stitched and grimly shook her head. "If only character could pay my bills."

"Leave the poor woman alone and put those idle hands to better use." Mama shooed Jen away.

Having Warner in the house did ease the situation over Luke. Mama was going through one of her long spells of silence, but everyone made an effort to be polite and keep up appearances. In spite of the tension under the surface there was a feeling of relief when Luke went to work in the dusty law offices of Thomas O'Connell. When he was at home he still spent much of his time shut up alone in his room, but occasionally he and Ella walked out together. Jen wondered if he was trying to make up to her for his mother's unkindness. Even though Mama had apologized, relations had been strained between the two women since Easter.

"Mama! I've scorched my hair ribbons!"

"Stop fussing." Jen handed Maybelle the new red ones she had planned to wear herself. "You can have these."

Everyone was up early on Decoration Day. Breakfast was eaten on the run. Mama heated flatirons for last-minute touch-ups, and the girls stood in sunlight to make certain no shadows showed through their skirts. Charles was sent upstairs to take off a torn shirt and put on his best. Gram, with the kitchen finally to herself, finished her toast and green gooseberry jam and poured herself a second cup of coffee. "A storm is coming; I can feel it in my bones," she said, even though the day shone warm and yellow through the windows. She never attended the Memorial Day parade. "Who needs to be reminded of sad things?" she asked.

In the front hall Papa was at the tall pier glass smoothing his lapels while Luke, standing behind, tried to catch a glimpse of the mustache he had started growing on his eighteenth birthday. It was a very handsome mustache, and Jen guessed that her brother thought so too.

"Charles, you have bootblacking all over your hands." Mama rubbed her temples as if she felt a headache coming on. "Hurry and scrub it off or we'll all be late."

"Pretty Girl? Aren't you feeling well?" Papa asked.

"I'm a bit under the weather," she admitted, "but I'll take a dose of bromide before we leave the house."

Jen hoped her mother wouldn't be ill; it upset her and made her feel guilty. Then something happened, a brilliant drop of time splashed forever into memory. Her father, still looking at the mirror, saw something in it that nearly stopped his breath. "Why Ella . . ." he murmured. "You're not in mourning."

A luminous figure stood in a haze of sunlight by the window at the landing. "I couldn't wear black another day . . . I just couldn't." Ella hesitated, her face golden beneath a white bonnet trimmed with a deep splash of blue, her embroidered dress of snowy batiste showing the beautiful curves of her bosom and hips. "Louisa?" she asked, "Do you think it's all right?"

"Yes," Mama said. "It's all right." Papa and Luke stared as the young woman, her face bright with relief, came down the rest of the way. Mama did something rare and unexpected. She reached out and lightly stroked Ella's cheek. "You look so lovely, my dear." Jen was sure that any hard feelings between them must have dissolved at that touch.

The day was hot and humid by the time they reached Aurora, and Main Street was crowded with people waiting for the parade to begin. Charles and Maybelle streaked off in opposite directions, but Jen, anxious about her mother, stayed close by. Mama often suffered from a mysterious female complaint, but Jen knew better than to mention it.

There was so much she wanted to ask, so many things that she needed to know, and yet it was so difficult to get answers. Not long ago a frightening thing had happened; she had awakened one morning to find her nightgown stained, blood seeping slowly from her body, and had been sure she must be dying from some humiliating disease. It was hours before she could bring herself to mention it to her mother.

"It's the curse." Mama was too embarrassed to look her in the eye. "It happens to women and adolescent girls once a month. I'll show you what to do."

"A *curse*? Like a mummy's curse? Some sort of evil spell?"

"Don't be so silly, Jen. A nuisance is what it is."

"But why does it happen?"

"It just means that you're capable of bearing a child, that's all."

"I am? That's *all*! Why, Mama — it's a wonder!" Jen grew more and more excited now that she knew she wasn't dying after all.

"It's nothing to rave on about, believe me."

"But when will it stop?"

"Not for years and years . . . until you're middle-aged."

"Then that means that *you* still . . .?"

Mama grew even more flushed. "I've always had a difficult time. So if you suffer from cramps or backache, I have some medicine you can take."

"How old were you when it first happened?" Jen wanted to know.

"Almost sixteen. I was terrified . . . and so ashamed. My mother was dead; there was no one to talk to or turn to. When I married a year later I didn't even know . . ." Flustered, she stopped, and then went on. "You must be careful not to exert yourself during the monthlies. And you mustn't wash your hair."

"Mama . . . if you knew it was going to happen to me soon, why didn't you tell me?"

"Nice people don't talk about such nasty things until they have to."

Jen was curious. "Does Papa know?"

"We've never discussed the matter. And you must never mention it to anyone." Mama ended the conversation by quickly leaving the room.

Later Jen decided that the business wasn't as bad as all that. She felt no particular discomfort, and she was awed, even elated, to think that she was mature enough to carry a child. Yet she was still deeply puzzled. How a baby was actually conceived was something she only vaguely understood and wasn't entirely willing to believe. Jessamine Doyle was the only authority; she had looked through her father's medical textbooks and told some of the girls things that

they were sure she had made up just to shock them. Jen
didn't think Jessamine had enough imagination to invent
all the tales she told, so there must be some truth to what
she said. There were such large gaps in her own information. Fascinating areas of human experience weren't
supposed to be discussed, and she would have to find them
out for herself. She didn't ever intend to suffer from the
female complaint the way her mother did, and when the
time came and Maybelle was old enough to understand,
she would prepare her little sister in advance. Maybelle
wouldn't like it, but Jen wasn't going to let the child be
frightened if it could be avoided.

16

An Unexpected Meeting

The Memorial Day parade was led by a cornet band, the instruments flashing silver in the sunlight as the marchers passed beneath banners of evergreen, past the snapping salute of hundreds of flags. The Aurora firemen followed, the volunteers stepping briskly in their cream and scarlet uniforms.

"Look — there's Lukas!" Ella waved her handkerchief, straining to see. "Doesn't he look splendid!"

Behind her, Jen heard gossipy Mrs. Roth murmur to a friend, "Look at the bold thing flaunting herself, with her husband barely cold in his grave."

She turned, whispered indignantly, "Ella's allergic to black. It makes her break out in big red blotches." She was satisfied when Mrs. Roth kept her sharp tongue to herself after that.

A patriotic float rumbled by, draped with bunting, with some ladies of the Eastern Star posturing on top, gazing heavenward as if they were all dying stoically of war wounds. During the lull that followed, Jen, glancing across the street, saw Davey Sawyer standing with his aunt among the crowd. It was the first time she had seen him since the night of the sleigh ride.

"Davey!" she called. "Dave — ey!"

"Jen, do stop that racket!" Mama put a hand to her head.

Float followed float, with long spaces between, and more bands, and another corps of volunteer firemen from Wilson's Corners. Then two young veterans from the Spanish American War came into view, one with a wasted, jaundiced face and the other hobbling by slowly on crutches. Jen had read in the *Echo* how these local boys had followed Theodore Roosevelt up San Juan Hill in '98, but to her they looked pitiful and not heroic at all. And even though she felt sorry for them, she wished they could move a little faster. She was very anxious to get across the street.

"Jen!" Davey had seen her and was trying to get her attention as a carriage full of bowing dignitaries went by. "Wait for me after the parade!" Then the Grand Army of the Republic, with Asa Gentle on a prancing black horse and a group of sweating foot soldiers, came between them. As the stout, graying men, bursting out of ancient blue, brass-buttoned uniforms passed by, the spectators grew silent, awed that these familiar marching men had survived the terrible battles almost four decades ago. Jen waited, impatient to see Davey. As the parade wound up the street, the crowd fell in behind; boys fired imaginary rifles at each other and fell from invisible injuries, while the girls and women lifted their skirts from the dust, tilted their parasols against the streaming sunlight, and strolled off in the direction of the park.

It was almost a stranger that Jen greeted. The laughing, healthy boy had changed into a gaunt, hollow-eyed young man with sharp cheekbones in a pale face. What was recognizable was the glad smile, the shock of thick hair, the warm, green-glinting eyes.

"Jen, you look so good. Different, though. It must be the hat."

"Do you like it?"

"It's a wonderful hat. Except it covers up your hair." They fell into step as the drumbeat tapped away into the distance.

Jen said, "I tried to see you lots of times, but your aunt wouldn't let me. I hope she gave you my messages."

"No messages. But she did give me the drawings you sent, the ones of Rheba Watson raiding the saloon." Davey laughed. "I think those did me more good than all of Doctor Doyle's horrible remedies. I'm sorry about my aunt, Jen. She's peculiar in some ways, but I know that her nursing saved my life. I'm truly grateful to her."

The Eldorado gleamed under a fresh coat of white paint. Baskets of ivy geraniums swung in the breeze along the graceful porches. Jen, feeling the familiar enchantment of the place, told Davey happily, "Someday I'm going to dance here in the ballroom."

"With me or Willard Roth?"

"Davey . . ." She touched his arm. "I wasn't spooning with him the night of the sleigh ride."

"I know. Not that I blame him for trying."

They entered the green shimmer of the park. Blue jays and orioles, cardinals and scarlet tanagers splashed their vivid colors through the vaulting elms and aged oak trees. A crowd had collected on a point of land jutting above the

blue sparkle of Lake Tuscarora. Each grave in the Soldiers'
Cemetery was decorated with a wreath and a tiny flag, but
Jen found it difficult to think of death in such a radiant,
sunlit place. Charles often played among the lichen-crusted
tombstones, making a game of war, but today they would
be reminded that men were buried here who had spilled
their lives in real and deadly battles.

There were speeches, prayers, and recitations. The
Congregational church choir sang a hymn, and Mary Frances
Howard, a bouquet shaking in her hands, recited "Cover
Them Over with Beautiful Flowers." Jessamine Doyle was
overcome with emotion and carried away in a faint. As Jen
and Davey stood side by side their hands accidentally brushed
and then clung. The girl felt a rush of pleasure. For a time
she was hardly conscious of anything else. Then, as her
father stepped to the podium to give the Gettysburg Address, she tried to pay attention. Each year his thrilling
delivery touched the spectators, making her feel proud.
She looked at all the attentive faces turned toward the
speaker, at Charles and Maybelle in the front row, at
Mama, wearing a different expression, one that Jen recognized from the wedding portrait on top of the piano. It
was a mixture of shy pride and expectation, combined with
a hesitant sadness in the blue-gray eyes. Apart from the
others, Luke stood gazing at Ella's golden profile serenely
lifted under the filmy hat, and he looked as if he were
discovering again what he had seen when she came down
the stairs in the morning. *How beautiful they are*, Jen thought.
Powerful feelings welled up, flowed out through the tips
of her fingers, touching Davey and including him. He

smiled down at her and tightened his warm hand around hers.

Reverend Williams. pink with heat, bowed his head and intoned the last resounding prayer, and the ceremony was over.

"Will I see you again soon, Davey?"

"I'll be back to school in a few days. Miss Barrett's been coaching me, trying to help me make up what I've missed so I can still pass the Regents exams."

Reluctantly their fingers separated. As he left it seemed to Jen as if the holiday went with him. She and the younger children walked home with their mother; Papa had stayed in town and Luke had invited Ella to take a cruise up the lake on the little steamer, the *Lady Aurora*. When they reached the house, Mama took a spoonful of pink liquid from a small brown bottle, and Jen realized that she was having one of her bad headaches. She followed her mother upstairs, covered her with a light blanket, and put a cool folded cloth on her forehead. "Shall I pull down the blinds?"

"Yes, please."

"It was lovely, wasn't it . . . when Papa gave his speech in the cemetery?" Jen came back from the window to linger by the side of the bed.

"Your father has a clever way with words." Mama sounded tired.

"Did you see Davey Sawyer? He's feeling better now. He'll be back at school any day."

"I thought he looked a little peaked still."

"Is there anything I can get you? Any way I can help?"

"Just leave me for a while, Jen. I need to be alone."

17

A Coming Storm

The day flattened oddly. There was a brooding silence in the house. Above the hot calm in the yard clouds piled steadily in the metal-colored sky.

"You must never speak to me again like that, Francine!" *Whack!* Maybelle had set all her dolls in a row on the wooden glider on the back porch. "Or look at me in that naughty way, Florinda!" *Whack! Whack!* "And you, Rose Marie, must sit in the corner for being such a bad, bad girl!" *Whack! Whack! Whack!* As Maybelle prayed over them, Jen thought it was no wonder the dolls looked so pale and wide-eyed and alarmed. She hoped her sister wouldn't one day inflict on her children the awful punishment she pounded into her toys.

She played horseshoes with Charles, and then they both threw sticks for the dog, but Rock could never find the sticks to fetch and Jen soon grew bored with the game. While Charles and Gram played cards, (nobody could ever beat Gram unless she let them), Jen went up to her room for pencil and paper to try and sketch the Decoration Day ceremony. With quick movements she drew her father at the podium, the listening figures among the tilted tombstones, a wink of bright water in the background, but none of it pleased her. The outlines were there, but something important was missing. She brought out her old paint box and dipped the brushes in water. This time, color brought the scene to life, as blue and scarlet birds streaked through green branches, flashing strokes of red sent the *Lady Aurora* steaming up a cerulean lake, and gay squiggles of pink and purple, green and yellow put people giddily in motion through the park. When it was finished she felt a rare sense of satisfaction with what she had created. She had captured a fragile thing, the essence of the shining moments when Davey had held her hand in his. Now she had this to remind her. Excited, she looked in on her mother. "I thought that you might like to see this." She held out the picture for inspection.

Mama held her throbbing head. "Very nice, Jen." She closed her eyes. "I think I can sleep now. You'll help Gram with the supper?"

"You know I will."

Laughter rose from the hall as Luke and Ella arrived home with Papa. Jen went slowly down the stairs. In the kitchen she helped Gram set out the big platters of baked ham and fried chicken, the salads and pickles and deviled eggs, while the younger children carried the food out to the table under the trees. The air was stifling; thunder mumbled in the distance.

"You said it would storm. How come your bones are smarter than mine?" Charles asked his grandmother.

"They may be smart, but they never helped me out much in school." Gram chuckled. "Now let's eat before the rain comes and ruins our meal."

They ate quickly. Jen couldn't get into the mood of a holiday picnic. Luke was quiet and Papa thoughtful as he scooped out vanilla ice cream from the old wooden freezer. Then Ella, who had come home in such high spirits, suddenly began to cry.

"Why, what's the matter, girl?" Papa asked.

"Those horrid women . . ." she said, weeping. "Whispering behind my back because I wasn't wearing mourning clothes."

"Never you mind." Papa came and sat beside her, put an arm around her shoulders. "It's how *you* feel that counts. You've looked back long enough . . . Now it's time to look ahead."

"Jamie's right. You let go of those tears . . . just let them go," Gram advised.

"I'm glad you put that ugly dress and that black hat away," Charles said. "Now you look like a bride again."

Ella cried harder at that. Papa mopped at her face with his handkerchief, pushed back the damp hair from her forehead, and lightly kissed the tip of her nose. "There, dear. Better now?" It was the same tender voice he used when he called Mama Pretty Girl, and it made Jen feel peculiar. "How would you like another nice cold glass of lemonade?"

"Oh, James . . ." Ella sounded sleepy and content as she leaned against him with her arms around his waist. "It's so nice to be held again . . . so nice." She looked up at him, not crying, but with lashes still wet with tears. "You are the nicest, dearest, warmest man I know."

"This stuff is melting." Jen saw that Luke was as uncomfortable as she was. Even angry, as he passed the ice cream around.

"Why don't you go in and play the piano?" Papa asked Ella. "You know that always cheers you up."

"Perhaps I will after we take care of the dishes."

"Never mind that. And never mind jealous old women. You look beautiful today . . . just like your old self again."

"James, you always say exactly the right thing." Ella's smile was radiant. "Maybe I cried because I felt so alive today, and it scared me a bit."

"Here comes Mr. O'Connell," Luke said.

Their visitor carried a bottle of whiskey, which he presented to Papa. While Luke went into the house to get tumblers, the lawyer pulled on a branch of spirea and a shower of bright new pennies poured out into his hands. "What happened to your diamond engagement ring?" he asked Ella after he had distributed the coins among the children. As she stared in astonishment at her unadorned finger, he reached into the pocket of Charles's shirt and found it there. Then, to the little boy's great disappointment, the three men went to sit together on the bank of the river. Jen had never before seen her brother taste anything stronger than cider. She hoped her mother wouldn't come downstairs and see him drinking liquor.

Later, after the dishes were washed and while Ella played softly on the rosewood piano in the parlor, Gram swung with Charles and Maybelle in the wooden glider. It made a lonesome, squeaking sound. Jen, sitting alone on the porch steps, felt out of place. She was too old to be rocked and too young to join in the adult conversation. She wished she could hear what the men were discussing. Politics, probably. Mr. O'Connell and her father were Democrats in a largely Republican township, and they liked to complain about the way the government was being run whenever they got together.

> *"Drink to me only with thine eyes,*
> *And I will pledge with mine . . ."*

Ella's voice floated from an open window —

> *"Or leave a kiss but in the cup,*
> *And I'll not look for wine."*

It was a wistful English air that made Jen feel lonelier. She went into the house to look in on her mother. Upstairs, in the shadows of the bedroom, Mama slept restlessly, her long copper hair spread across the pillow.

When she came down again Mr. O'Connell had gone and Papa sat by himself on the porch steps. Jen sat with him, smelling the fragance of his aftershave and the scent of alcohol that lingered in his mustache.

She said, "It gives me shivers when you give that speech."

"It was written the year I was born," he told her, "and I expect people will be repeating it long after I'm gone." The tip of his cigar glowed in the fading light. "Lincoln fascinated me when I was in school and he still does. His wit and wisdom . . . his tolerance and compassion have always inspired me. It saddens me sometimes to know that he was often a melancholy man . . . and so harshly judged in his time."

"You won your gold medal speaking about him, didn't you?"

"Yes." Papa puffed and exhaled. "Such a long time ago. It was an important night. People expected big things of me after that. Some even predicted I'd become a famous orator or politician or statesman, but I had just met your mother at a church social, and nothing else seemed that important, then."

"I think you *are* a great man, Papa."

"*Jen*." He laughed. "I'll never measure up to your high opinion of me."

She leaned against him, hoping he would stroke her hair as he used to, but instead he stood up and tossed his cigar into the yard. "Have you looked in on your mother?"

"Just now. She's sleeping. I missed her at supper."

"So did I. I only wish . . ." He didn't say what it was that he wished, but the longing that was always in him surfaced in a long, sad sigh. "I guess I'll go into the parlor and sing with Ella for a while."

Jealousy flared, then quickly went. Why shouldn't he have some pleasure on his holiday? Soon his fine tenor mingled with Ella's soprano, the voices beginning, then breaking off again as they practiced to improve their harmony. It was good to hear the music and their laughter as the glider squeaked back and forth, back and forth. "The babes are in dreamland," Gram said at last. "Come on, Jen . . . you can help me take them up to bed."

The Storm Breaks

Luke stood silhouetted among the dark trees swaying above the river. Jen strolled across the lawn to join him. She was surprised to find him still drinking whiskey. Uneasy, she broke the silence between them. "Do you like working for Mr. O'Connell?"

"It's all right."

"You don't sound very excited about it."

"You think I should be enthused? Clerking in a law office when out there — " he waved vaguely toward the rushing water and beyond as lightning glared white across the tossing branches — "is something so big, so bursting with life and vitality . . . that I can hardly stand the thought of it."

She had never heard him talk like this before, his voice loud, almost rude.

"Things are happening out there, Jen," he said, "important things. Artists are painting pictures of it, architects are designing buildings for it, engineers are spanning bridges over it . . . and inventors are dreaming up machines that will bend this country out of shape." Furiously his words lurched on, "And here *I* am, with the wheels in my head spinning, and I'm not a part of it — I'm not going any-where — that's what's driving me crazy!"

"If you feel this way," she said, "then why don't you leave?"

Luke emptied his glass, tossed it down into the soft grass. "And let him have her all to himself?"

"What are you talking about?"

Luke laughed, a mean laugh, not like his own. "You notice things."

"Like what?" Her scalp tingled and her heart gave quick, hard, warning thumps.

Silence.

"You mean Papa . . . and Ella?"

Silence.

"Is that what you mean?" Yet she didn't want to hear what he had to say. "You know he only cares about Mama."

"You think he's so perfect," Luke said. "So *wonderful*."

"He is! You used to think so, too."

"Well, he isn't. I've *seen* . . . and I *know*."

"What have you seen? What do you know?"

Luke turned to her, and she saw that what had been building in him since suppertime was about to explode. "That summer when Mama was so sick . . . remember?"

How could she not remember that curious time when their mother had shut herself off in a world of her own and lay upstairs not speaking, barely eating, not even able to get out of bed? Doctor Doyle couldn't tell them what was wrong, except to blame her illness on nerves. Ella had left, there was too much for Gram to do, and so Papa had hired Hilda Bjorness to come and help out at the house.

She was big-boned and awkward, a country girl of eighteen
or nineteen with her buttons done up hit or miss and yellow
hair spiraling down from a makeshift knot. Gram, usually
so tolerant, constantly found fault and made her sleep on
a pallet made up in the parlor. Yet Jen recalled Hilda's
warmth, her fresh primitive beauty. Her teeth blazed white
in a rosy face, and her eyes were a dark, peaceful blue.
In a time of confusion she emanated comfort, and when
Charles cried at night for his mother Hilda lulled him to
sleep against the soft fullness of her breasts.

"Yes, I remember."

"It was hot that summer . . . too hot to sleep." Luke's
voice was quiet now, almost a whisper. "One night I went
downstairs and saw them . . . Hilda and Papa . . . *together*.
They didn't see me and I never told, but the queer thing
is that next morning Mama got up for the first time in
weeks and said, 'That woman *goes*.' "

Now Jen knew. Papa had done something so wicked and
unforgivable with the hired girl that Luke had stopped
loving him. Her eyes burned; sadness filled her throat,
making it difficult for her to speak.

"You saw him tonight," Luke said. "You saw what kind
of man he is. Why, he couldn't keep his hands off Ella."

She hated her brother for saying these cruel things. "Ella
was feeling bad. She just needed someone to be kind."

"Not *him*!"

"Maybe you're jealous."

He grabbed her wrist, wrenching it. "Take that back!"

She wanted to hurt him as much as he had hurt her.
"I won't! I think maybe you want Ella for yourself!"

The singing voices inside the house had died away. Luke dropped Jen's wrist. "I'm going in there now."

There was a sharp crack of sound and a flashing of light, and then the rain swept in, cool and fresh, across the yard, driving Jen in after him. In the parlor Ella sat sorting through a pile of sheet music with Papa behind her, his hands resting lightly on her shoulders. He looked up and smiled as the brother and sister came in. "Good. Now we can do some four-part harmony."

"Shouldn't you be keeping Mama company?" Luke asked. "You know she isn't feeling well."

"Well, Ella and I . . ." Luke stumbled against the piano stool, "are going for a walk."

"Lukas, don't be so silly. Can't you hear? It's raining!" Drops spattered briskly against the windows as Ella began to play again. "Shall we try 'All Through the Night'?"

On top of the piano Jen saw the old-fashioned wedding photographs in the oval golden frames joined by a single hinge. There, in the beauty and innocence of their youth, her mother and father faced each other. But something had happened to them in the intervening years, some deep disharmony that would never be set right again.

Only Ella was singing. Her voice faltered, then stopped. "What's the matter?"

"I'm going to call it a day, dear." Papa's hands dropped to his sides. "Turn in early. Rain on the roof always puts me to sleep. 'Night, son." He leaned toward Jen to give her his quick goodnight kiss, but she stiffened and moved out of reach.

"Anything wrong, Jen?"

Without a word she turned and fled up the stairs to the safety of her room.

"Jen . . . wake up."

It was her brother, bending over her, his hand on her shoulder. "What is it?"

"Shhhhh." he whispered. Luke's face was bleak in the early dawn. "I haven't slept yet. I drank whiskey last night for the first time, and it made me kind of crazy. I want you to forget what I said."

"As if I could!" Angrily she pulled away. Beside her, Maybelle groaned, grinding her teeth in her sleep.

"Jen, please. I never intended for you to find out about Papa. I can't tell you how sorry I am."

"Sorry? You *liked* saying those horrible things! You're *glad* that I know!"

"That isn't true! I never felt so bad about anything in my whole life!"

"I hate Papa for what he did," Jen whispered fiercely. "But I hate you more for telling me!"

Luke rubbed his hands wearily across his cheeks, his shoulders slumped in despair. "I know how you must feel," he said, "but believe me . . . I never meant to hurt you like this."

She turned, huddled away from him. Outside birds were waking, breaking into song as he quietly left the room.

19

A Walk Down Main Street

June was a time when summer stretched out further than
the eye could see, with the Glorious Fourth just hidden
round the bend. Peddlers traveled around the county hawk-
ing fish and vegetables and tinware, and the first auto-
mobile anyone in Aurora had ever seen spurted down Main
Street at twelve miles an hour, wagging a long tail of
barking dogs behind and causing an almost hysterical excitement.

It was a time when the Baptists stood in the river with
their clothes on and were saved, although none of them
seemed in much danger of drowning, and a Wild West
show came to town and stayed two days, causing small
boys to break out in bucking bronco fits that lasted weeks.
Rheba Watson staged a Temperance Rally under a canvas
tent with live specimens of repentant drunks, and a viola-
shaped woman from Cleveland spoke at Pickwick Hall,
offering improving lectures on Ideal Girlhood, Ideal Womanhood, and Ideal Motherhood, open to females of sixteen
or older. Jessamine Doyle lied about her age and was admitted, but Jen couldn't see any improvement in her after.
"I didn't mind missing out on the lectures," she told Mary

Frances, "because things with *Ideals* attached are usually exceedingly dull."

In June, she helped her mother put up dozens of jars of strawberry jam. It was the start of a strenuous season of pickling and preserving that would continue late into the autumn, through raspberries, currants, cherries, plums, peaches, pears, apples, and grapes. Jen hated the scrubbing and sterilizing of the glass containers, the feverish heat of the kitchen where the great stained jelly bag leaked tart juices into a shining copper kettle. Yet on winter days she loved going into the shadowy fruit cellar and finding summer magically distilled in row upon row of those radiant jars.

She was shelling peas from the kitchen garden one hot afternoon when Luke burst into the house waving an envelope and calling for Mama.

"Son, what is it?"

"I've sold a short story! It's going to be published in the *Addison Review*, and they've paid me three dollars for it!"

"Three dollars!" Mama was incredulous. "What kind of a story?"

"It's called 'A Walk Down Main Street.' " Luke flung himself down at the table, red-faced and perspiring from the long run home. "It's about a boy growing up in a small town like ours, and the people who live there . . . and work . . . and dream . . ."

Mama asked, "But who would want to read about people like that?"

"There's a growing interest in realism now." Luke spoke

enthusiastically. "It's in the air . . . It's happening in all the art forms. The country is coming of age, Mama — growing up! I think a lot of people are ready to discover the truth about themselves." He kept glancing at the check in his hand as if he couldn't believe it was really his.

Jen didn't say anything. She never spoke to Luke at all now unless she had to.

"So this is what you've been doing in your spare time." Mama asked, "And when may we read this wonderful story?"

"I'd rather you waited and saw it in print. But I want you to understand that it isn't really about Aurora or the people you know . . . The place and the characters are imaginary, of course."

"Thank goodness for that!" Mama was growing more and more excited. "I can't wait to see it!" Jen felt envious. Nothing she ever did pleased her mother that way. It only made her resent Luke more.

"Well, Jen . . . aren't you going to congratulate your brother?"

"What's so special about getting a story published?" It satisfied Jen to see the look on Luke's face; it was like Papa's when she had put away her birthday hat. "It doesn't suit me anymore," was the explanation she gave, but she could see how puzzled and offended her father was when she took out the childish straw with the streamers to wear once again. Was it because she was hurt so much herself that it was easier to cause pain to someone else? She wondered.

🦋

A time of endings and beginnings. River Road thickened with dust as the summer folk arrived to open up the big estates. The sound of shears snipped busily across the quiet afternoons as gardeners preened the shrubs and fussed among the flower gardens. Jen felt something in her quicken to the playful *pock pock* of tennis balls echoing from the clay courts and the carefree shouts of the players, as if she were suddenly attuned to some rich, vibrant music that had been performed before, but that she had never really heard until now. Why did some people have so much, she wondered, and others so little?

"There!" Charles said on the day that classes ended. He heaved his worn boots into the closet. "I'm not putting those things on my feet again until September." He smiled happily at his bare feet and hopped, skipped, and jumped across the room.

"What about Sundays?" Maybelle reminded him. "Every single Sunday, Charles."

"Sundays don't count." The Sabbath was the numb spot in his week, a day of rest for someone who was never sleepy in it, a day when he sat and squirmed in hot, tight clothes while in his imagination he stripped and went in swimming. He wished he could be like Luke, who had stopped attending services altogether, dropped out of choir, and even given up the Wednesday evening prayer meetings. Reverend Williams had come twice to the house and tried to coax him back into the fold, but Luke couldn't be persuaded. Since then his mother's pride in him had changed to shock and disapproval.

"It's a scandal and a disgrace," she said when Luke

wouldn't go to church with the family. "I lay the finger of blame directly on that man."

"Mr. O'Connell has nothing to do with this." Luke flared up. "It's my decision, and there's no reason for you to get riled."

"I am riled! You've changed, and I don't like it. Rheba tells me that you've been stopping in at Dewey's. And what about that book that I found in your room?"

"I have dozens of books in my room," Luke said through his clenched teeth.

"*Sister Carrie*, it's called. Oh, it sounds pure and innocent enough, but when I looked inside the covers I was horrified. I'd like to know where you find such trash."

"I'm lucky to have it. There were only a few hundred copies of this novel published, and a friend of Mr. O'Connell's sent him one from New York."

"There!" she cried. "What did I tell you about that man!"

"It's the most exciting book I've ever read in my life. Mr. Dreiser writes about life as it is!"

"It's *disgusting*! I'm ashamed of you for bringing it here where your sisters might see it. I won't have it here in the house."

A younger Luke would have sighed and obeyed her wishes. Now her angry adult son shouted, "Then I'll read it somewhere else," and slammed the door as he left, with the novel jammed under his arm.

20

The Glorious Fourth

She awoke to the rattle of gunfire in the yard. Not gunfire, Jen realized sleepily, but firecrackers. Charles always sent up the Fourth of July with a bang. Next to Christmas it was the most important event of the year. As she lay in bed dreamily contemplating the wonders ahead, Charles rushed in and pounced. "Get up, Jen! Don't you know what day this is?"

"Yes, I know! It's Wednesday, silly!"

"Not just Wednesday — it's the Fourth of July!"

"Poor Charles." She patted his head. "You've made a terrible mistake, dear boy. It's only the third."

An awful doubt wavered on his face, then cleared away. "No, it has to be the Fourth. Ask Papa — he's putting up the flag. And hurry up, or everything will start without us."

Still she teased him, pulling the covers over her head and snoring while he pummeled and pestered. Finally she leaped out of bed with a laugh and Charles ran away down the stairs.

Jen went to the window. Gulls flowed serenely above the silky mist rising from the water. The morning sky was light and mild; soon it would be a vivid, burning blue. It was perfect weather. But wasn't it always this way on the Glorious Fourth? She wanted to stretch and savor every minute of the celebration.

Her clothes had been laid out the night before. Now she dressed quickly in a blue-and-white-striped shirtwaist and a navy skirt that Warner had made over for her from one of her mother's silk dresses. Her face sparkled back from the oval mirror as she brushed her hair with long, firm strokes. Then, standing sideways and pulling in her breath she decided yes, Madame Bonnomo's exercises were definitely showing results. Suddenly she felt like Charles, afraid that the holiday would start without her. As she hurried down the stairs she felt a moment of giddiness that she knew must be excitement because a moment later it was gone.

Gram was at the cookstove basting eggs with bacon fat. The smell made Jen feel queer.

"Where's Mama?"

"The poor dear's feeling poorly." Gram clicked her tongue in sympathy. "Now find your father and tell him that his breakfast is ready."

He was on the front porch with Maybelle, gazing up at the Stars and Stripes as the flag billowed in the morning breeze.

"The Glorious Fourth . . ." Papa had a gorgeous way of rolling the *r*'s around in his mouth. "Be thankful, girls, for all the blessings Old Glory confers on you. There is no greater country, no grander flag, no prouder day." He always talked this way on special occasions; as a child it had filled Jen to bursting with patriotic pride. Today his remarks sounded pompous, even foolish, to her. "Gram says to come and eat." It was difficult to look at him, to speak naturally. She turned and went back into the house, deciding to skip breakfast. She had no appetite this morning.

Upstairs her mother lay propped against pillows sipping tea. Jen said from the doorway, "Gram says you're feeling poorly."

"It's just my old kidney complaint. I've taken pills for the pain."

"I'm sorry." Jen wondered why a day that brought so much pleasure to so many people could cause her mother such suffering. "Then you won't be coming with us."

"I'll just lie here and rest. The peace and quiet will do me good. You'll have to take my place."

"Nobody can take your place. It won't be the same without you." One of Mama's hands, roughened from housework, lay open on the sheet. Impulsively Jen picked it up and kissed the callused palm. She wanted to tell her mother that she loved her, but she knew the words would annoy and embarrass her. Yet she needed something to make the day right again. "Mama . . . how do I look?"

The elusive fingers slipped away. "Handsome is as handsome does, Jen."

"But I really need to know."

"You look nice enough. Now run along and help Mrs. McAlister."

Nice was not a nice word at all. It was empty and polite, Jen thought as she went down the stairs, and she didn't care if she ever looked *nice*. There was a stir and bustle in the hall where Ella, in full pink skirts and a tight bodice, was straightening Luke's cravat. It annoyed Jen to see her brother's pleased smile showing under the tips of his thick golden mustache as Ella hovered around him with her eager, touching hands.

"Why, Jen," the young woman sang out, "you look all grown up and absolutely bee — utiful!"

Even though it was what she needed to hear, Jen resented Ella for speaking the words she had wanted her mother to say.

There was a moment of suspense as Charles, whose feet had expanded with freedom, tried to squeeze them back into his old boots.

"If they won't fit, Charley-boy," Papa said, "then we'll just have to cut off the ends."

Charles was gleefully horrified. "Of my toes?"

"Of your shoes, you ninny." With a hard tug Papa managed to get them on. Gram hurried down the stairs in her polka-dot dress and old-fashioned bonnet, carrying a parasol to poke out of the way anyone who might spoil her view of the parade. "Come on, everyone! Let's go!" She was always the first one ready on the Fourth of July.

Horses and carriages streamed toward Aurora from every corner of the county as they rode with their neighbors in a democrat wagon. The four little Haight boys glistened from an extra mid-week bath, their scrubbed heads smelling of tar soap, the youngest wriggling in Ella's lap as she hugged him all the way to the village. The streets were lined with men wearing straw hats, women in light summer dresses, and children, still starched and shining, with waving flags in their hands. Flags were everywhere, hanging from poles and from porches, swagged over shop fronts, waving brightly above the town hall, the opera house, the red brick school.

"There's Mary Frances!" Jen pushed through the crowd to reach her friend. Just as they met she saw a familiar blaze of red hair flickering in their direction. "Quick, let's duck. That awful pest Willard is heading this way."

"He's looking for me." The girl's plain face burned with a fierce proud blush. "I've promised to spend the day with him."

"With Willard?" Jen was baffled. "But why?"

"He's nicer than you think." Mary Frances was now a furious pink. "And don't think he cares about you, any-more — not after the way you've treated him. He's a very sensitive individual, Jen. It's a pity you've never learned to appreciate him."

Using both elbows and stepping on feet to clear his path, the boy arrived to grab Mary Frances by the arm and lead her away. Remembering all the things she'd said about him in the past, Jen hoped that she hadn't hurt her best friend's feelings. But recalling the even worse things the other girl had said about Willard, she couldn't help laughing.

It was almost noon. The baking day had fired the sky a deep ceramic blue. On the lookout for Davey, she walked toward the Eldorado.

"Jen, I have to go — *now!*" Charles, jumping up and down in distress, tugged at her arm.

"Didn't I tell you to do that before we left home?"

"I did. That was ages ago . . ."

Quickly she pointed out where he was to go and then continued on along the noisy street.

The hotel, its broad front doors flung open, gleamed like a wedding cake under a gloss of bright sunshine. Stylish men and women lounged on the wide verandahs; from the dining room came a murmur of voices and the silvery clink of tableware. Jen waved to Mr. Hammond, the elegant owner, who was strolling down the slope toward the dock where the steamer was berthed. A child in a sailor suit rolled a hoop across the clipped green grass and Jen remembered how, when she was small, she and her barefoot friends had envied the children staying at the Eldorado. How incredible those boys and girls had seemed, blazing in white as they played croquet on the lawn with their nursemaids, children who never got dirty or had to do chores.

"The parade is starting any minute!" Maybelle ran up, yanking Charles along after her. "Come on — Gram's saved a place for us!"

Still Jen lingered, thinking of the privileged guests registered at the hotel. Her parents had never taken a vacation together except for that odd little honeymoon years ago when they had stayed with old Aunt Rose.

"Jen, hurry!" Charles begged.

She didn't intend to stay shut within the tiny boundaries of home forever. Luke had talked of thrilling happenings far beyond Aurora, and one day she would go and see for herself. Maybe years from now she would return and sit on the porch of the Eldorado and wave graciously to old friends passing by: like Willard and Mary Frances, pushing a red-headed baby in a wicker pram. The thought made her smile.

"It's starting! I can hear the music playing!" Maybelle wailed.

"Come on, then." Jen took her brother and sister by the hand.

21

A Declaration

The Fourth of July parade, a glorious mishmash and muddle, was led down Main Street by a noisy German band. Plump men in short leather trousers, fat knees pumping up and down and red cheeks swollen with effort, were followed by the Drum and Bugle Corps, acrobats and clowns, minstrels in blackface, and a lengthy caravan of fraternal floats.

"Didn't you see Papa?" Maybelle pointed as the Benevolent Order of the Elks swept past. "He smiled right at us."

Jen waved as the mayor rode by. Willie Virkus had been run out of town once for some forgotten offense, but that was before he had made a fortune with his famous Gargling Oil ("Good for Man or Beast") and come back all dressed up like a diplomat to have the last laugh. The carriage full of politicans was followed by a tableau of girls in filmy red, white, and blue dresses, posing in a patriotic trance, and by the Congregational church choir booming out "The Battle Hymn of the Republic." Then came the terrific reverberating drumbeat of a marching band from an adjoining township, renowned for the vast quantities of beer it took each year to quench its monumental thirst, and the procession was over.

"The best parade ever!" Gram waved her parasol in her enthusiasm.

Jen laughed. "You say that every year."

Everyone headed off into the lazy green spaces of the park where each family would claim its own territory for the afternoon.

"I found us the best place of all." Charles had run on ahead and was back to guide them to the spot he had chosen.

From a rise of land above the lake they could see the busy panorama of the scene below, where women spread clean cloths on the tables, men in shirt-sleeves stood around the flowing kegs, and children darted in and out among the trees. Somewhere out of sight the German band played on with a cheerful *oompah oompah*, and nearby three little girls dancing in a circle toppled breathlessly into the long soft grass.

"How did you celebrate the Fourth of July in Pittsburgh?" Maybelle asked, as Ella unpacked the picnic hamper.

"It wasn't anything as nice as this. Leland and I usually went to some fancy place to eat and then we'd go dancing. Leland was light on his feet for a heavy man."

Jen saw jealousy stare out of Luke's eyes at the mention of Ella's married life.

"He adored good food. I must confess that I was a poor cook. Rosie tried to teach me some of the simple things,

but I'm sure I disappointed my husband in that depart-
ment."

Papa had joined them. Now he smiled across the table.
"I doubt if he minded whether you could cook or not. To
him you must have been

> 'A lovely apparition, sent
> To be a moment's ornament; . . .
> A dancing shape, an image gay,
> To haunt, to startle, and waylay.' "

"James, what a perfectly lovely verse." Ella's cheeks
were rosy with pleasure.

"Wordsworth's old-fashioned," Luke said. "When it comes
to love poetry I think Swinburne can write rings around
him."

"Then you'll have to prove it to me." Ella's teasing mouth
turned up at the corners.

Softly, he recited:

> "If love were what the rose is,
> And I were like the leaf,
> Our lives would grow together,
> In sad or singing weather,
> Blown fields or flowerful closes,
> Green pleasure or gray grief;
> If love were what the rose is,
> And I were like the leaf."

There was a strange little pause. Gulls wheeled, crying overhead as the German band played on in the distance. Ella's eyes were dazed as she stared at Luke with her mouth slightly open; tiny beads of moisture glistened on her nose.

Charles burst out, "I know a better poem than that!

The world is so full of a number of things,
I'm sure we should all be as happy as kings."

"And indeed we should." Gram snatched him in against her polka dots. "I am . . . aren't you?"

Everyone talked and laughed as salads and sandwiches were passed around the table. In spite of the heat, cold chills passed through Jen's body. Hadn't Luke just declared himself, openly admitted that he was in love with Ella?

"Why aren't you eating?" Maybelle asked. Jen shrugged; the sight of food made her queasy.

They had taken Ella in when she needed them, when there was no place else for her to go. Now Papa and Luke were competing for her easy smiles and affectionate touches. For a moment Jen wondered if she could be imagining this. No, Luke's feelings were there for anyone to see on his handsome face. Papa was harder to read; he was always gallant with women, but Jen was certain that she saw behind his eyes a fascination for Ella. He had betrayed Mama once. Why not again?

"Honey, you're a million miles away." Ella's light fingers touched her cheek. "Aren't you feeling well?"

Jen's emotions were hot, tangled. Didn't Ella realize how

wrong her behavior was, how dangerous? "I'm just not hungry, that's all."

Papa looked worried. "You haven't been yourself for a long time. What's wrong, dear?"

Jen's eyes filled with tears. She shook her head, unable to speak.

"Leave her alone. Jen's been busy growing." Gram leaned her cheek against Papa's sleeve, and Jen saw that he was still her little boy and that she would always love him best, no matter what. She wished that she could be as simple and accepting. But she would never forgive him for what he had done — or trust him not to do it again.

22

Winners and Losers

"Hurry up, son." Eustace Bean, the stout, bearded captain of the volunteer firemen, came up behind Luke and thumped him heartily on the shoulder. "The tug-of-war is about to begin, and our honor is at stake." He winked at Gram. "Last year the team from Wilson's Corners won the cup, and they vowed they'd never give it back."

"That bunch of sissies?" Gram gave Luke a little push. "Well, go get it!"

He turned to Ella. "Are you going to come and watch?"

"We'll all go," Papa said.

As she waited for the contest to begin, the bright sunshine made Jen's eyes ache. She wondered where Davey was and wished he would show up. There was noise and confusion. Dogs ran barking up and down the field, Sousa tunes marched briskly from the bandstand, firecrackers popped and crackled. A man with a megaphone shouted that the children's competition would begin shortly. A large crowd had gathered, trading jokes and good-natured insults with the opposing teams. The starting gun was fired. Faces contorted, puffing and blowing, the firemen swayed back and forth as they pulled the thick rope in opposite directions. There were cheers and jeers as the groaning men from Wilson's Corners gained an advantage, a big-bellied man at the end giving them the ballast they needed.

"Harder, boys . . . *heave* . . . *heave*," urged Eustace Bean, panting, while Luke strained at the end of the line, his hair wet, his muscular bare arms gleaming.

"Pull, Luke — pull!" Gram cried, and spectators moaned with suspense as the teams struggled backward and forward. Then, with an unexpected surge of power, the Aurora volunteers, slowly and steadily, dragged their opponents across the line. A triumphant shout went up with a hundred hats as Eustace Bean, glowing with heat and victory, accepted the silver cup filled to the brim with beer, drank deeply, and passed it along to the thirsty contestants. The big-bellied man had collapsed in the dust and was helped to his feet. Luke wiped the foam from his mustache and ran to the sidelines.

"Lukas, how strong and splendid you were!" Ella wiped the dirt and the sweat from his face with her handkerchief, as if he were Buttercup, Jen thought with indignation, and still five years old.

"Jen, will you come and watch the races?" Charles looked nervous. He had practiced a whole year for just one event, and she knew how important it was to him.

"Of course I will." As she walked with her brother and sister to the far end of the playing field, where the smallest children were already stumbling and sprawling in their attempts to win the blue, red, and white ribbons, she thought again of Davey and wondered where he was. What if he didn't show up at all?

"Egg and spoon race . . . eight-to-ten-year-old girls!" bawled the man with the megaphone. Shrieking youngsters swirled around him, scrambling to take their places.

"Why don't you enter?" Jen asked Maybelle.

"I never win at races."

"Hurry up, little lady . . . we're waiting for you," an official called out.

"Go on . . . *try*." Jen pushed her sister toward the starting line.

As the gun went off and a mob of intense girls wobbled away, the egg toppled from Maybelle's spoon. Tearfully she hurried back to stand with Jen. "There! I told you I never win at stupid games."

"You'll do better next time."

Maybelle sulked. "There won't be a next time."

As the competitions went on Jen was aware of Charles standing quietly beside her, not moving or speaking. When the hop, skip, and jump contest was announced, he made a queer little peep in his throat. "This is it, Charles." She gave his hand a squeeze. "Your big moment. Go on, now." Still he hesitated. Boys were lining up, one behind the other, pushing and shoving.

"He's afraid he'll come in last," Maybelle said, with a scornful glance at her brother. "Like he did last year."

"I am scared," Charles took a deep, shuddery breath. "But I'm going to win." He took his place at the end of the line and Jen saw how small and fragile he was compared with the bigger, stronger boys. As they competed she grew even more discouraged. Then it was his turn. Charles looked in her direction. She nodded and tipped up her thumbs. The child stood very still, concentrating, collecting himself. Then he hopped, skipped, and jumped. There was silence. No one was quite sure of what they had seen. An astonished judge ran to measure the performance; the boy had landed an incredible distance away. Charles, his thin chest heaving, ran back to stand with his sisters.

"First prize — " the judge shouted — "Charles McAlister!"

"You did it! You really did it!" Jen cried as the official pinned on the award.

"I wish Mama had been here to see me."

"Never mind, she'll be so proud of you! Now go find Gram and Papa quick and show them that beautiful blue ribbon!"

"Next year," Charles said, still gasping for breath, "I'm going for the high jump." Jen smiled as she pictured him vaulting over sofas and chairs for the next twelve months.

The three-legged race for younger girls had been called, and big-boned Elsie Claffin, in dingy gingham, was looking for a partner. Her fierce eye fell on Maybelle. "Come here, you. You're going in this one with me."

"I never win at races," Maybelle squeaked.

"You're going to win this one," Elsie promised, "or you'll wish that you had." She clapped a hand over Maybelle's wail of protest, dragged her to the starting line, and gave her a hard shake to warm her up. When the race began, Maybelle, pinned like a splint to her determined partner, lurched up the field in record-breaking time to finish far ahead of the others.

"There, aren't you glad you entered?" Jen asked, as the little girl limped back with the first prize ribbon fluttering on her chest. But even in victory Maybelle was morose. "Don't you dare tell Mama my partner was Elsie. She'll be sure I'll catch something awful." Everyone knew that the Claffins had lice. "And I hurt my ankle, too. It's probably broken."

"Now it's our turn." A smiling Juanita Flatt held out her hand to Jen. "Will you enter with me?"

"I'm game if you are." They giggled as their legs were bound and giggled as they floundered up the field, the tall, thin girl attached to the short, wide one. Then Juanita tripped and the two of them flopped over in the dust, still laughing helplessly, unable to sort themselves out.

"Need a hand?" It was Davey Sawyer, grinning down at them.

"What I really need," Jen said, delighted to see him, "is one less leg. Right now I have three."

He helped them up, brushed them off, and offered to buy them both lemonade, but Juanita shyly refused and ducked away. Thirstily Jen gulped down the icy drink. "I'm so glad that you're here. I was beginning to think that you wouldn't come at all."

"A wheel fell off the wagon about five miles out of town, and it took forever to fix it."

Slowly they walked through the park. A speaker was shouting from a distant podium as they moved in the direction of the lake. From the bluff above the water they watched bathers running up and down the shore below, the women in dark serge dresses and long black stockings and the men in skinny two-piece woollen suits. Jen sank down in the grass and wrapped her arms around her knees.

"Once when Luke and I were small we took off all our clothes and jumped into a field pond. I'll never forget how good that water felt against my skin. Of course my mother found out. She said she could understand a boy doing such a thing, but not a nice young lady, and she made me promise never to do it again."

"But you'd like to."

"Yes, I would." Jen lifted her collar at the back so that the wind could flow under her hot, heavy hair. Far out on the lake tiny sailboats fluttered past with clean handkerchief sails.

"Do you always do what your mother tells you to do?" Davey teased.

"I try but I never feel I can please her. She's so sure of what's right and wrong, and she can always quote a scripture to prove it. Often my ideas are exactly the opposite of hers. It's like that tug-of-war I saw today . . . both of us pulling in different directions." She sighed. "Sometimes she says that I'm stubborn and hardheaded."

"Are you?"

"I must be. She never lies." Jen smiled down at Davey as he stretched out beside her and folded his arms under his head. His thick hair shone amber in the sunshine. "You look well again," she told him. "Have you been working hard?"

"Not as hard as I'd like to. My parents are too careful

with me now. Not just because I've been sick, but because of what happened to my brother."

Jen knew that an older brother had died.

"It was four years ago," Davey went on. "Daniel stepped on a pitchfork in the barn. At first it didn't seem too serious, but it was. It was agony for him . . ." Davey shut his eyes against the light. "And for us, to have to watch him die that way. Now they only have me to worry about, and they worry a lot. My father won't let me help out as much as I should. He's older now, and not that well, and it bothers me."

"You love him a lot, don't you?"

Davey opened his eyes. There were flecks of gold floating in the clear green, Jen noticed. "He's my father. Why wouldn't I?"

"I don't know." Jen probed bleakly in the grass, searching for four-leaf clovers. "I don't feel that way about mine anymore."

"Why not?"

She hesitated, wanting to put her feelings into words and yet thinking it would be disloyal if she did. Davey put a hand on her wrist. "I'd never repeat anything you told me. But don't tell me anything if you don't want to."

She wanted to talk. Ever since Memorial Day she had needed to find a way to release some of the sadness. "Papa did something bad a long time ago, and I found out. I can't ever forget it. I used to think he was so wonderful, but now I see him as he really is, and it hurts."

"That's growing up, isn't it? Seeing things as they are?

Adults are always trying to keep things secret, but children eventually understand. Jen, I like and admire your father. Everyone in town does. When times are hard and people need him, he never lets them down."

"Other people. What about Mama? What about me?"

"Whatever he did," Davey said, "I know he must be sorry for it."

"There's more to it than that. Something is happening in our house . . . Everything is changing. Ever since Ella came it hasn't been the same."

"If it's any help," he said. "I'm here. I'll always listen."

She looked down into his smooth, tanned face. A powerful impulse made her raise his fingers to her cheek, then bend her head to touch her mouth lightly to his. Shocked by the sensation they pulled apart, staring at each other. Then he drew her face to his again, her dark hair spilling around them, shutting out the sunlight.

"Jen!" Maybelle ran towards them, followed by Charles. "Gram says that she'll buy us tickets for the *Lady Aurora* if you'll take us!"

The boy and girl rose from the grass, not looking at each other, suspended in discovery. Shakily Jen asked, "Davey, will you come too?"

It was late afternoon when they arrived back at the picnic grounds. Women were rounding up their families for supper; crying babies were shushed and rocked and fed, and children were sent away to find their fathers. At the kegs men sent back word that papa would be right along, then they had another glass, told one more story.

"See you later, Jen?" Davey had promised to join his parents at the Gentles'.

"I'll meet you at the pavilion." After food and festivities, speeches and competitions, ball games and concerts, a magical evening still lay ahead, with dancing and fireworks beneath the summer stars.

23

At the Pavilion

Casey would waltz with a strawberry blonde,
And the band played on.
He'd glide 'cross the floor with the girl he adored,
And the band played on . . .

Laughing couples circled the floor of the breezy pavilion; children spun gaily with children, husbands with wives, sweethearts dreamily dipped and swayed beneath the colored lanterns.

"Looks as if she aims to catch another husband mighty quick." Mrs. Bean, watching with a friend beneath the trees, couldn't take her eyes off Ella Landers. "My Eustace only danced with her because he pities the flighty little thing."

"Now Jamie McAlister's feeling sorry for her, too," said Mrs. Pole. "He's as graceful as he ever was, and so youthful yet. I was sweet on him in my time, but he never cared for anyone except Louisa. It's a shame the way *she's* aged . . ." She nudged Mrs. Bean with her elbow. "If I were her I wouldn't welcome that one under my roof."

If Davey had heard the women talking nearby, he gave no sign and Jen didn't ask. As the band glided into "It's

Three O'Clock in the Morning," a melody that Jen had often heard drifting upriver from the Eldorado, the tall, slender man and the small, golden woman waltzed around and around in perfect step, Ella's full pink skirts lifting in a whirl of embroidered petticoats.

"You aren't going to let our Ella steal the whole show, are you, young man?" Gram had arrived with Charles to watch the dancers.

"I've only danced one time, Mrs. McAlister," Davey told her, "and that was when the old bull got loose and trapped me up in the north pasture. I swear I did steps then that haven't been invented."

"Then let's see some. Jen's not too bad herself, you know. And when she's finished she can pass you along to me."

"I'll dance with you, Gram," Charles offered.

"Will you, young fellow? Something kicky is what I like, and a tune with a bounce to it."

"That's what I like, too." Charles walked off arm in arm with his grandmother.

There was scattered applause as the waltz ended. Jen watched as Luke crossed the floor to where his father stood with Ella. "He's going to ask her to dance," she guessed.

"He looks nervous," Davey said.

"He ought to. Luke doesn't know the first thing about it."

The music started up again. Jen was sure her brother had never held a woman in his arms before. Yet, as the couple swirled past, the pink streamers at Ella's waist spinning in the wind, she was surprised to see how well he was doing. Davey was, too. "I thought you said he couldn't dance."

"Luke learns fast when he wants to." Jen had never seen him look so happy, as if he held a dazzling gift that he never wanted to set down. She looked for her father and found him standing close by with Thomas O'Connell and Bessie Trowbridge, passing a flask back and forth among them. Bessie drank hard liquor and smoked cigarettes like a man. Because she was living in sin Mama said she could never set foot in her house, but Jen didn't believe the woman was really bad. Bessie was rich round curves and high strong color, and Jen was fascinated by her orange hair and rouged cheeks and ripe, ready laugh. Some of Jen's best sketches were of her, although she was careful not to let her mother see them.

Again the music stopped. As partners were exchanged, Papa headed unsteadily up the steps of the pavilion. Jen could tell by Luke's expression that he wasn't going to give Ella up to his father. She was relieved when the young woman slipped her arms around both men and steered them away from the dance floor to a lemonade stand nearby.

"Would you like to take a chance with me?" Davey asked. "Your brother made it look almost easy."

"I would. And it is."

"I'll have to keep an eye out for my parents. They think any kind of dancing will send me straight to hell."

Jen wondered how anyone could decide what was right or wrong when everybody had such different notions. In spite of the objections Mama raised to all sorts of things, she had never said a word against dancing. The answer, she supposed, was to do what seemed comfortable, the way Davey did. He knew that going around in circles for a few minutes wouldn't lead him astray, no matter what his folks preached. As the band played "Tales from the Vienna Woods," he tripped over his feet and hers as they maneuvered gingerly around the crowded floor. "Guess that old bull didn't teach me much after all."

"You're doing fine." Jen encouraged him by counting *one two three* over and over under her breath. They were both laughing as they stumbled to the end of the waltz, but even when the band stopped playing Jen's head went on spinning.

"Lukas, show your sister what a good dancer you are." Luke and Ella had come back to the pavilion. "And I'll let this handsome young man hold me up for a while."

"Me?" Davey was bashful but not unwilling. "I'm afraid it will be the other way around."

"Jen doesn't want to try her luck with me," Luke said.

"Of course she does," Ella insisted. "Don't you, honey?"

Jen couldn't think of anything she wanted to do less as she and her brother waited for the music to begin. When it did they moved awkwardly and in silence. One of the members of the band stood up to sing:

> *"After the ball is over,*
> *After the break of morn,*
> *After the dancers' leaving,*
> *After the stars are gone —"*

Jen knew the poignant words by heart:

> *"Many a heart is aching —*
> *If you could read them all.*
> *Many the hopes that have vanished —*
> *After the ball."*

"Loosen up," Luke said. "You're stiff as a board."

"So you're an expert now, I suppose."

"What's the matter with you?"

"Nothing's the matter with me. You're the one making a fool of yourself, mooning over Ella for everyone to see. What would Mama say if she saw you carrying on this way?"

"Carrying on!" Luke turned Jen so abruptly that she almost lost her balance. "You know something? You sound just like her . . . setting standards, passing judgment. How I feel about Ella is my own business."

"It's wrong, Luke. You musn't — you can't! She's years older, and she's family."

"Must not, cannot . . ." Once again he turned Jen so roughly that she stumbled. "She's not related. And what difference can three years make between a man and a woman anyway? If something possible has just occurred to me, I'm not going to let you or Mama or any town gossip make it *im*possible. Stay out of this, Jen!"

He stopped dancing. Angrily brother and sister glared at each other as couples veered past, trying not to collide with them. Ella circled by and Luke reached out to seize her arm. "I think we should change partners now."

"I don't want to dance any more," Jen told Davey when they were paired together again. "Please . . . may we go?"

They walked down from the lighted pavilion into the soft dusk beneath the trees. Jen heard her name called and saw her father coming toward them. "I'm going to go on home now and see how your mother is feeling. You be sure and ride home with the Haights after the fireworks."

"I will, Papa."

"Don't worry about her, Mr. McAlister," Davey said. "I'll look out for her."

"I know that you will . . ." Still the man seemed reluctant to leave. "Are you two having a good time?"

"Yes!" they said together.

"I thought so." He reached out and touched Jen's hair. "You looked as if you were. Everyone seems to be having a very good time." He stared at the dancers, following their movements with a faint smile. "Remember when you used to waltz with me, Jen?"

"Yes." Years ago she had stood on his great shining boots and let him lift her around and around the Turkey carpet, but she hoped he wouldn't ask her now.

"Goodnight, then." Jen was sure he had seen the reluctance in her eyes. She was ashamed and relieved to see him go.

Davey said, "He must be worried about your mother, not to stay and see the fireworks."

"It's not that. He just can't stand seeing Luke and Ella together."

"I'm not sure what you mean."

"It's too disgusting. And I hate him for it. I hate them all!"

"Jen, come here." Davey took her hand and led her into the shadows where no one could hear. Fireflies shimmered and vanished; far off they heard excited shouts as children tried to capture them in jars.

"The terrible thing is," she said, "that my father feels the same way about Ella as Luke does."

"You think they're both in love with her?"

"Yes!"

"Listen to me. Ella's a beautiful woman, anyone can see that. And the truth is that no man could help admiring her . . ."

Jen tried to swallow the hurt that filled her throat. "Are you telling me that you feel that way, too?"

Davey put his hands on her shoulders. "I enjoy looking at her. It was even fun dancing with her. But it's just a natural attraction . . . nothing more than that."

"It isn't natural with Papa. A married man ought to be loyal to his wife!"

"And he *is*. But how things ought to be and how they really are are two different things. Jen, you can't change human nature around just to suit yourself. I don't pretend to know how your brother feels about Ella, but I'm sure that you're wrong about your father." He lifted her face between his hands. "Don't try and sort this out tonight. We only have a little time left together, and then we won't see each other again for ages."

"I don't know what's wrong with me today," Jen told him. "But I'm sorry if I've spoiled things for you."

"I'm glad you told me what's bothering you. Now let's go watch the fireworks."

People were strolling toward the hill where the climax of the holiday took place each year. Lights sparkled in the darkness as the *Lady Aurora* floated homeward, the sprightly sound of a banjo clearly heard across the water. When they had cruised during the afternoon there had been hours and hours ahead, but now the day was almost over. Jen wished it wouldn't end so soon.

"Ahhhhhhhhh . . ." A sigh rose from the crowd as the first rocket arced high into the sky above the hilltop.

They stood apart from the others, Davey so close to Jen she could feel his warm breath on her hair. More rockets and torpedoes rose on luminous stems and bloomed briefly, fiery blossoms soaring higher, streaking tall enough to touch the stars.

"Ahhhhhhh . . ." The grand finale came at last, filling the acres of the night with an immense fantastic flowering.

"Jen?"

She turned and looked up as Davey bent to kiss her. The Glorious Fourth had ended. Yet, for the rest of her life, it would burn like a spark in her memory. Overhead the last dazzling bouquets scattered downward, drenching radiant petals into the lake.

24
Fever

"Mama says that you're to come downstairs. Now."

It was Maybelle, looking scared and guilty as she hovered in the doorway.

"Why?"

"Best come and see for yourself."

Jen sat up and groped for her robe. It was a little after nine by the dented brass clock at the side of the bed, which meant that she had overslept. Then she remembered that it had been almost morning before she finally dozed off after a restless night. Her limbs ached, there was a dull pressure behind her eyes. As she went barefoot down the stairs her head felt so strange that she had to grip the banister. Mama waited for her in the kitchen, looking bothered and serious. She waved Maybelle out of the room, then motioned Jen to sit down at the table.

"I've just heard something that's upset me. I have to ask you if it's true."

"If what's true?"

"Maybelle said that she saw you yesterday with the Sawyer boy, and that the two of you were . . ." Mama hesitated, a flush rising from her throat into the hollows of her cheeks, *"kissing* in the park."

"Yes." Jen looked her mother in the eye. "It's true."

For a moment Mama said nothing at all as she rubbed her thumb over and over the same worn spot in the oilcloth. Puss, in a rare moment of affection, came out from behind the stove to arch against the woman's skirt.

"You shouldn't have done such a thing," Mama said, looking grieved.

"Why not?"

"Don't play Miss Innocent with me! You go to church and Sunday school."

"We never talk about anything as interesting as kissing in church or Sunday school."

"You needn't be impudent! Haven't I tried to teach you children the importance of a strong character, of resisting temptation . . . of keeping a good reputation?"

"Yes, you have. But what does that have to do with this?"

"Everything! Kissing, Jen — and in a public place. I'm ashamed of you. Why didn't you think about what you were doing?"

"You can't think and kiss at the same time, Mama! Besides, it just happened. It didn't seem wrong."

"A good girl doesn't go looking for trouble."

"What kind of trouble?"

"A woman has a higher, finer nature than a man, Jen. A male is more animal and selfish and will always try to take advantage. You must never give in to their desires unless, of course, you're married. Then at times you must submit." She shook her head sadly. "Then it's your Christian duty."

Jen rubbed her forehead, trying to push the ache away. She was confused about what her mother was trying to tell her. "I didn't give in to Davey . . . The kissing was my idea. At least the first time," she said defiantly. "And I liked it both times! I thought it was fun!"

"Then you'll find out soon enough what that kind of fun leads to when you're married and have a husband in your bed night after night!" Mama's voice broke; she covered her mouth with her hand as if to push back the bitter words. "I want you to promise me there'll be no more of this foolishness."

Jen pulled the cat into her lap and buried her burning face in its fur, but Puss slithered away. "I can't promise. I like Davey. I know that I'll want to kiss him again."

Mama hit the table angrily with the heel of her hand. "You must give me your word. I don't want you to be alone with that boy."

"I'm sorry if you think what I did was bad. I know I've disappointed you again, but I won't make a promise that I might not keep."

"You're hard!" Mama cried out. "Hard and stubborn to worry me this way. You'll be sorry for it too, I promise you that!"

Jen sat with her head propped between her fists. A lovely experience had been ruined; she felt exposed and humiliated.

Her mother's eyes were worried, "You look so tired and pale this morning. What's wrong with you, Jen?"

"I'm sick," Jen realized. "Oh, Mama . . . I feel so bad."

🐦

It was a grim, debilitating disease. For the first few days Jen was restless and irritable, unable to eat or sleep as her temperature rose. Doctor Doyle came to the house and sat by the bed, gently probing her tender stomach, his kindly eyes concerned behind his thick glasses. "Typhoid," Jen heard him tell her mother, and then she lost track of time and place as she lay sweating and delirious. Her head throbbed with violent dreams; when she was conscious someone was there to put cool liquids to her lips, to replace the soaked bedding with smooth dry linen, to ask what she needed. The younger children were forbidden to visit, but sometimes Jen was aware of Maybelle's anxious face mutely asking something she didn't understand. Once she heard puzzling thumps, felt a moist nuzzling in her hand, and heard Charles in a far-off voice calling Rock out of the room.

"Please," her mother pleaded, "you must eat something to keep up your strength." Days had passed, her body had burned away into an ashy lightness, but Jen couldn't swallow the nourishing broth. It was hard to bear any weight as soothing hands bathed her. From the troubled center of her consciousness she felt a gentle pressure on her skull, heard a delicate slice of sound, and after that her head felt curiously relieved.

Gradually nights grew separate from days, the terrors and evil dreams became less real. Gram came, when the others had gone to bed, to sit and rock and croon the oldtime melodies. Always the familiar touch, the squeak of the chair, the same hopeful question, "Any better tonight?"

One evening Jen said, "I'm freezing, Gram. My bones feel like icicles."

"You've taken a chill. I'll put more covers on you."

"No, they're too heavy . . . they hold me down."

"Come here, then. In the rocking chair with me."

"I'm too big for that."

"Not anymore . . . there's not much left to hold." Gram scooped her easily into her lap, and wrapped her around with a light, cozy shawl. The motion of the rocker carried Jen back and back, into some safe haven of the past. "There now . . . better?"

"Mmmmm. I dreamed I was lost in a blizzard and nobody came."

"Didn't I hear you? Didn't I come?"

"Mama was looking at me through a wall of ice. I scratched with my nails, but I couldn't get through." It felt good to cry, to feel the warm melting comfort of tears.

"The bad dreams are almost over, lamb. You're getting well."

"Gram? Will you tell me about the time you ran off with the gypsies?" It was Jen's favorite story. All of them knew it by heart.

"For years after it happened my family claimed I'd been stolen away, but the plain truth is," Gram said, "that poor raggletaggle bunch didn't set out to steal a parcel of trouble like me. No, I went along on my own . . . Why, I begged them to take me! I must have been five or six then, old enough to know better, you bet! My folks had immigrated to Canada from the Old Country and tried their hand at farming up in northern Ontario, but those terrible cold winters froze up their ambition, and by and by they drifted down to the States, where they thought life was easier and

mellower. Hah! It was a restless time, people moving on
from place to place, hoping to strike it rich somewhere
else. My parents rented a nice farm hereabouts, and things
were going along and going along . . . are you all right?"

"Better, Gram." The chills had stopped. The lullaby
voice made her drowsy.

"Well, in those days I always wanted to be off on my
own, playing in the meadows, pretending. I was a sun-
flower ten feet tall sprouting yellow petals, or a red bird,
or a gorgeous butterfly sailing on the wind. I loved color
so — the way you do — and I wanted a purple dress more
than anything. I loved excitement . . . like firecrackers
going off in my head. Anyway. One day this funny old
wagon bumped past the house and meandered down the
road and stopped near a brook and right away I was warned
'Lacey, you stay away from that caravan, those are wicked
gypsies' and so forth and so on, and so naturally the first
chance I got I went over to see what was going on. And
fell in love with the whole crazy bunch of them. They
never had a single thing to do except have a wonderful
time."

"You sure like a good time," Jen murmured.

"Like someone else I know. There was always a friendly
racket going on and music playing and people dancing around.
And the men fished and hunted, and when they grabbed
a-holt of a rabbit or squirrel they skinned it and threw it
into this pot that simmered away day and night. And before
long I was dipping in my greedy hand and helping myself
and dancing like a lunatic when I felt like it."

"I don't suppose your folks knew what you were up to."

"You suppose right. And when my mother's best Irish lace tablecloth disappeared from the clothesline I never said a word, not even when I saw one of those dark-skinned lovelies wearing it as purely as a bride. How I loved the way those women rattled and glittered — and the things that went on over there!"

"What things?"

"The eating and drinking and laughing and singing and gambling. That's where I picked up my knack with cards. It was life, juicy and delectable, and I was part of it! But one day I found the gypsies packing up to leave, everyone excited to be going down the road and nobody caring at all about leaving me behind with the bones and the rubbish. I cried as if my heart would break and begged them to take me, and since nobody minded one way or another I climbed on the wagon and went."

"Didn't you say good-bye to your parents?"

"I never gave it a thought, that's the sort of rosebud I was. But after I'd been missing for a while and caused a great ruckus, the new pastor recalled seeing a fair-skinned child on top of a caravan singing at the top of her lungs, and my father tore after us and by the time he caught up the gypsies were as glad to give as he was to get."

"Were you punished?"

"What do you think? In those days folks showed how much they loved you by scraping the skin off your backside every chance they got."

"I'd rather be licked than have typhoid fever," Jen said. "That's how I was punished."

"For what?"

"Kissing Davey Sawyer."

Gram stopped rocking. "Now who put that ridiculous notion in your head?"

"Mama said I'd be sorry for what I did, and I am. I didn't know it was such a bad thing to do. Maybe because it felt so good."

The chair rocked back and forth again. Gram said, "Well, I've been kissing people all my life, and I can't recall a single instance where it ever harmed a soul. Now I know Louisa has a different slant on things, but the kissing she objects to is the kind the Claffin girls go in for."

"No, she thinks all of it's disgusting."

"She's afraid of her feelings, Jen. That's how it is. But love is a mighty force that has to flow. Dam it up, wall it in, and such human misery results. Your mother's a wonderful woman, but things happened to her when she was a girl that wounded her as surely as if she'd been crippled or maimed."

"Like what?"

"Her father was a tyrant in his house. Louisa was deathly afraid of him and no wonder. I suspect he raised his hand against her and her own sweet mother many a time. She couldn't love that man . . . She must have hated him."

"How awful." Jen couldn't bear to think of it. "But I'd never hurt her," she said. "So why can't she love me?"

"Is that what you think? Why, she loves you more than words can say, and she shows it every day in a hundred ways. But don't ask more from her than she can give. There's more to love than kissing, my girl. Just remember that she'd die for you, and so would I. Now I want you to

go to sleep, and when you wake up in the morning things
will seem a whole lot rosier."

"Rosier!"

Jen, looking in the mirror for the first time, saw what
she must have known but been afraid to discover. During
the worst phase of her illness all her hair had been cut off
close to the scalp. "How could you do this to me!"

"Believe me, I didn't want to, but I had to," Mama said.
"Unless the hair is cut before it falls out from the fever it
never grows in as nice as before. Yours will be as thick
and grand as it ever was, just wait and see."

"I'll be an old maid or dead before that happens!"

She stared, unable to believe anyone could look so hid-
eous; black eyes sunk into deep purple pockets, dry skin
blotched with brown, and only an inch or so of limp lack-
luster hair framing the starved and bony mask that was
her face. Injun hair, Maybelle had called it. Except this
time it was the Injun who'd been scalped.

She cried after her mother left the room, mourning the
loss of her crowning glory, her only glory, she thought.
Pinning up long hair into a shining twist or knot was the
mark of young womanhood every girl longed for. Now it
would be years before that day arrived. It was her own
fault, too. Hadn't she bargained with God that if Davey
recovered from pneumonia she'd give up her dearest possessions? Thinking of Davey brought on a fresh wave of
tears. She knew he admired her hair, and now he would
think she was the ugliest girl in school, in the village, in

the entire country, without knowing that he was, in a way, responsible. Life wasn't fair!

Ella brought a letter with her supper tray. It was a note from Mary Frances that made her feel even worse than before.

> *Dearest Jen:*
>
> *I was so distressed to hear about your getting typhoid fever. You must be going crazy cooped up in this heat wave. I ask your father about you all the time, and he told me the terrible news about your hair. I know I could never bear the loss of mine; I'm sure I'd rather die. I saw Davey Sawyer in town on Saturday, and he looked so dreadfully shocked when I told him you were bald! Willard says sometimes the hair never grows back. What a catastrophe that would be! Well, I hope to see you in high school if you return.*
>
> *Devotedly,*
>
> *MFH*
>
> P.S.   *Willard sends his condolences on hearing of your tragic state.*

Jen cried, "Everyone *knows*!"

"Honey . . . friends are friends no matter what," Ella said.

"That's easy for you to say!"

"Dear, I've kept everything that your mother cut off and made you the most beautiful braid. When it's pinned on nobody will know the difference."

"*I'll* know. This is absolutely the worst thing that has ever happened to me."

"You only lost your hair. You could have lost your life."

Jen said furiously, "Don't go preaching at me." She was angry with her father for telling the whole town about her calamity and with Mary Frances for spreading the news; she was sick and weak and ugly and jealous of every glowing hair on Ella's head.

Calmly, Ella dipped a spoon into a bowl of blancmange. "Now I want you to eat some of this. It's high time you were getting your strength back."

"I hate it."

"Please, Jen . . . do as you're told."

"I don't have to do what you tell me to do. I can't swallow that horrible stuff."

Ella brought the spoon to her lips. "*Eat it.*"

"*I won't!*"

"Did it ever occur to you — " Ella's voice was cool — "that we might be tired of waiting on you hand and foot, sitting up with you night and day?"

"Nobody asked you to."

Ella said, "It isn't that I minded, Jen. We were all glad to do it. But we're a little worn out just now, and the least you can do is cooperate." Once again she raised the spoon.

"So eat."

"No."

Ella dropped the spoon back on the tray. "Then please excuse me. I have more important things to do."

"Like falling over Papa and Luke? Don't think they care about you. They just feel sorry for you, that's all!"

Frightened and ashamed, Jen was sure for a moment that Ella was going to heave the pudding right in her face. She knew she deserved it. They glared at each other, hating each other. Then Ella quickly left the room. After she was gone Jen forced herself to eat all the blancmange as her penance.

25

A Departure

Something was happening.

Something dark, a quivering conspiracy that Jen could sense but not define.

Furtive whispers in the hall, hurrying footsteps on the stairs, a potent secrecy emanating from the walls of the house. For days she had been left alone for longer and longer intervals. People seemed weary and distracted, unwilling to answer her questions. Now, with the world coming back into focus again, she realized that she had not seen her grandmother for some time.

"Where is she?"

"I've already told you." Coldly, Ella picked up the supper tray. She came in as little as possible, stayed briefly, left quickly. "Gram's a bit under the weather."

"What's the matter with her?"

"It's probably just indigestion."

"She never gets indigestion."

"We don't know what it is." Irritably, Ella left the room. Jen, lying back against the pillows, wondered what was going on. Was she being protected from something? Through the half-open door she saw a figure lingering in the hall, staring at her close-cropped hair. "Charles!"

"I'm not allowed in there."

"I know. Just tell me what's wrong with Gram."

"She's sick."

"What does the doctor say?"

"I'm not supposed to tell."

He didn't need to. His solemn, frightened face revealed the truth. Now she knew. It was a dread of death flapping loose in the house that she had sensed. They believed Gram would die and had kept her from knowing. Because she was still an invalid, or because they held her responsible? From below Maybelle called up, "Doctor's here!" and from the top of the stairs Mama answered, "Send him right up."

It was early evening. The village bells tolled seven times. Through the open window Jen heard the ringing life of the cicadas, a clatter of birdsong, the rattle of carriage wheels along the dusty road. Carefully she climbed out of bed, avoiding the sight of her wasted legs and arms as she pulled on a robe. Then she crept barefooted into the hall, where Charles and Maybelle stood in silence outside their grandmother's room.

"You can't go in there," Maybelle said.

Defiantly Jen turned the knob and looked in, expecting to be scolded and sent away. Instead Mama said quietly, "Come in and shut the door. We were just going to fetch you. The doctor says it's right that you should be here now."

Gram lay in the carved black-walnut bedstead, her hair like fine silver webs on the pillow. Her eyes, half-open and unblinking, were turned toward the small squares of light at the window. Doctor Doyle held her wrist, feeling her pulse. Luke and Ella stood on one side of the bed, and Mama and Papa on the other. Jen's heart banged fiercely, and her knees were trembling with fatigue.

"Is it typhoid?"

Glances were exchanged. Papa said, "These things just happen, dear. Nobody's blaming you. We didn't want to upset you when you were finally doing so well. And your grandmother was holding her own until today."

"She took a turn for the worse this afternoon," Mama said. "We've sent for Reverend Williams."

"She won't want that," Jen told her. "She doesn't believe in all that."

Luke pulled the cane-backed rocker close to the bed. "Sit down, Jen . . . Save your strength."

"I don't want to sit." The room was hot, packed with the close, powerful scent of camphor and wool, eucalyptus and peppermint. A thrust of sweetness, too: someone had placed a spray of yellow roses in a jug on the commode. Everything was orderly, all the scattered possessions neatly in place. Jen resented Mama for tidying up Gram's life. Her grandmother liked clutter. Why didn't she sit up and send them away? None of this was possible or real. It was playacting, all of them taking solemn parts. Even Gram was pretending as she lay breathing roughly, her eyes gazing steadily toward the window. "I have to tell her something."

Papa shook his head. "It's too late for that, Jen."

"I have to."

The doctor rubbed the bridge of his nose where his glasses pinched. "I've always believed," he said quietly, "that the hearing is the last to go. I think that she knows that you're here even though she's unable to respond. So go ahead . . . Now is the time for all of you to speak to her."

Luke bent the bright tangle of his hair to his grandmother's breast, spoke quietly, kissed her brow. Ella did the same. Then Mama pressed the old woman's hand against her own cheek, keening "*Mrs. McAlister . . . Mrs. McAlister*" in a way that made Jen tremble. She watched her father huddle by the bedside, asking something or telling something to his mother that Jen couldn't hear. With surprise she noticed a faint white spot at the back of his head where his hair had thinned out. As he straightened, his mouth twisted in an effort to control himself. It was then that Jen understood that one day she would say a final good-bye to her own parents. It was a truth she had always known and yet never believed until now.

The doctor held her elbow steady in his hand. It was her turn to take leave of her grandmother. Her knees shook so much that they almost gave way. She put her lips close to Gram's ear. "I'm sorry . . . so sorry." She waited for an answer, some sign of forgiveness, but there was only the movement of the woman's chest rising and falling, the broken rhythm of her breathing. Ella slipped an arm around Jen's waist. "Honey, she's going peacefully. The doctor says she's not in pain."

"I want her to know that I'm sorry!" Jen struggled to

free herself. "It's my fault! She kept me warm when I dreamed about the ice!" Urgently she spoke: "Gram, don't leave . . . I love you! Please don't leave!"

There was a loud knock. Charles's voice wavered at the keyhole. "I want to come in there."

"You wait downstairs with Maybelle until you're called," Mama told him.

"But he's kicking me!" It was Maybelle. "He's kicking me ferociously!"

They heard the boy's sobs trail away. There was a change, a quickening in Gram's labored breathing. Jen had the sensation of time speeding up, of her own racing heartbeat, of cicadas screaming in the yard. Then came a gush of sound, a silence, then a long faint empty sigh.

"It's over," the doctor said. "I'm sorry, but she's gone."

Luke and Ella came together, his wet face blurred against her yellow hair, her small hands fanning out against his shirt. Mama, dry-eyed and silent, reached out her arms to Papa, supporting him as he leaned against her, crying like a child.

Over. Gone. Where? With the wind, with the gypsies, into Mama's safe harbor of souls? Only a replica remained, the eyes closed and hands serenely folded at the breast. Jen saw with wonder that what had been truly Gram had taken leave, that the miracle of her life was now enclosed by the large sealed mystery of death.

Sometime after midnight Luke came into her room. Jen was huddled in the rumpled bed, afraid of what lay beyond the dark.

"Are you awake?" he whispered.

"Yes."

He sat down beside her. "Are you all right?"

Finally she answered. "I feel so scared . . . and alone."

"I know."

"Gram always made me feel safe."

"And now you know," Luke said. "Love isn't always safe. Sometimes it's hurt and risk and loss. I saw your face in there today and I heard what you said . . . But it isn't your fault that she died. You must never believe that."

"She caught the fever from me, didn't she?"

"We don't know how these things are spread yet, Jen. If Gram took a chance it was because she wanted to. *She* was responsible, not you."

"I can't believe that she's *gone*."

He said, "I used to feel jealous sometimes, because of the closeness between the two of you. If I was supposed to be so wonderful, then why did she love you best? I could never figure it out." He paused for a moment, and then went on. "Now that I know I'm *not* so wonderful, I understand. The two of you were so alike. The strong feelings, the sense of fun, that lucky way you leap at life. Gram passed her colors on to you, Jen . . . the best part of herself . . . and so she can't really be gone, now can she?"

26

In the Parlor

In a room that was seldom used except for special company, Gram was the honored guest. Everyone helped with preparations for the wake. Jen, still weak from her illness, was excused from the scrubbing and housecleaning, but she fixed a mourning wreath for the door and arranged the flowers that Maybelle brought in from the yard, while Charles ran endless errands. Thomas O'Connell delivered a large glazed ham that Bessie Trowbridge had baked, and Mama, touched and confused by the generous gesture, went out of her way to be kind to him. The sideboard in the dining room was covered with pies and cakes as people came to the house from miles away. "You've always been there for us," one sun-browned farmer's wife said gently to Papa. "It's only fitting that we should now come to pay our respects."

The funeral was held at home. At the last minute Luke opened windows that were usually shut to let some fresh air circulate around the stuffy, crowded parlor. Jen, squeezed between Charles and Maybelle, glanced at the floral patterned walls, the stiff draperies, the ornamental knickknacks, and the collection of framed family photographs, but her eyes always skimmed back to the open casket where the body of her grandmother lay.

"I don't like this." Charles was too frightened to cry. "Gram won't like those people staring at her in that box."

"She doesn't know."

"She does so. She peeked. She opened her eyes a teeny crack just a minute ago."

"No, Charles," Jen told him. "She is really truly dead."

Maybelle's hands were clasped prayerfully in her lap; there were tiny blisters of sweat on her upper lip. "Gram stuck up for me," she said. "Now I don't have anyone on my side."

"I'm on your side," Jen said.

"You hate me because I told Mama that you kissed that boy."

"I don't hate you. But next time keep your mouth shut."

Maybelle sharply drew in her breath. "You'll do it again?"

"Shhhhhhh . . ." Jen whispered. "It's beginning."

Ella rustled to the piano, sat down, and played "O God Our Help in Ages Past" on the yellowed ivory keys. There was an outbreak of coughing and the sound of someone crying at the back of the room. Reverend Williams stepped up beside the coffin and mopped his face above his high, tight clerical collar.

> "*I am the resurrection and the life, saith the Lord.*
> *He that believeth in me, though he were dead, yet*
> *shall he live, and whoever liveth and believeth in*
> *me shall never die.*"

Papa's head was bent. He had been drinking quietly and steadily for two days, and Mama hadn't said a word. She sat beside him, her lips shaping the words as the minister spoke them, her head nodding in affirmation.

> *"In the midst of life we are in death; from*
> *whom shall we seek help?*
> *From you alone, O Lord, who by our sins*
> *are justly angered.*
> *Holy God, Holy and Mighty, Holy Merciful*
> *Savior, Deliver us not into the bitterness*
> *of eternal death."*

Charles kicked steadily at the rungs of his chair.

"Stop that," Jen whispered. Tears came to her eyes as he plunged his small warm hand into one of hers.

The service was brief. The minister didn't mention Gram's refusal to kneel at St. John's or to receive holy communion at the altar rail. Instead he praised her charity and laughter and celebrated her independent, joyful spirit. Sunshine poured through the parlor windows, touching all the solemn faces, glowing through the salmon-colored blooms of gladiolus. The body cushioned on white satin floated in a pool of light. Looking at the peaceful contours of the face Jen saw that whatever quarrel Gram had had with her Creator seemed now to be resolved.

What Mama had wanted was right, respectful, and most loving, and the preacher's words had eulogized a life with dignity, brushed it with beauty at the end.

27

A Scandal on Main Street

Warm September days and sparkling nights produced the richest harvest that the county had seen in years. Vineyards were draped with satin-purple, orchards glowed with peaches, ripening apples and a luscious green-gold weight of pears. At the depot in the village farmers waited in long lines to unload heavy bushels destined for city markets, and Mama, her hands stained dark with juices, finished the last of her jellies and jams.

On the first day of classes Jen stood in front of the pier glass, suddenly aware that she had grown at least another inch during the summer.

"Stop slouching," Ella told her. "Straighten up! Stand tall! Be majestic!"

"It's hard to be majestic without hair."

"Don't be silly." Ella wrapped a thick black braid around the girl's cropped head and piled it coronation-style on top. Even though it added a few more inches Jen could see it was becoming.

"It won't fall off, will it?"

"Of course not. It's pinned on good and tight. Now let me attach this red bow at the back."

It was good of Ella to fuss. Even though Jen always looked forward to school in the fall, getting ready this time had been hard. "I have butterflies this morning. What if everyone teases me?"

"Let them. In a day or so nobody will give it a second thought."

"Hair today . . . gone tomorrow?"

"That's better." Ella gave her a brief hard hug. "Now *keep* smiling, and you'll be just fine."

Maybe they would never be close again, but Jen was grateful that at least they weren't enemies, that she hadn't driven Ella away.

Mama was pumping water at the kitchen sink. Nervously Jen patted the shining crown at the top of her head. "What do you think?"

Her mother gave her a quick overall glance. "You'll do . . . except for that button coming loose. Thread a needle and I'll fix it for you while you're eating breakfast. A stitch in time saves nine, Jen."

"I know. I know."

It was such an important day. As she walked along the River Road with Maybelle and Charles, Jen felt a poignancy in realizing that some of her old classmates wouldn't be back. Higher education had always been a luxury for the rural children and she thanked her stars that Davey was able to return when village boys like Herby Pole were leaving to enter a trade, and girls like Juanita were needed to help out at home. Not everyone was as ambitious for their offspring as Mama. She had left after sixth grade to care for her sickly mother and because she felt that something in her had been stunted that should have been allowed to grow, she had promised that all of her children would have a secondary education.

"You're thinking about that boy, aren't you?" Maybelle said as they approached the familiar red-brick building. "You're wondering what he's going to think of you."

Jen didn't answer. But as she started to walk up the three flights to the lofty upper region of the high school, her sister, watching wistfully from below, called after her, "You look just like a queen!"

"I do?" The compliment sent Jen swooping regally up the staircase. "Why, thank you, Maybelle."

A cluster of students was waiting at the top. Mary Frances shrieked, "Jen McAlister! You're a sight for sore eyes. We didn't know what to expect!"

"She looks French," Willard said with a laugh. "*Trez chick*. And see, she's wearing the Eiffel Tower!"

"I think she looks mature . . . sophisticated . . . worldly." Davey appeared at Jen's side with a grin on his face and that was the end of the teasing.

"Did you mean what you just said?" Jen asked as they fell into step on their way to the auditorium.

"Of course I did. *But* . . ."

"But what?"

"One day, when I lose my hair, I expect you to say the very same things about me." They both laughed. The feelings between them were the same after all, even after the lonesome summer apart.

By the end of the week half the girls in the ninth grade had copied Jen's coronation hair style, and she no longer stood out from the crowd. There were too many other things to talk about. The *Echo* reported that three cadmium lights had been installed on Main Street, and Aurora crackled with speculation as to what the miracle of electricity would mean. "Imagine not having to heat all the water to wash the clothes," Mama marveled.

"Imagine having a hot bath instead of a cold one," Charles giggled. As the youngest member of the family he was always the last one into the tub on Saturday nights.

"Imagine having a bathroom in the house," said Maybelle. "And not having to go out in winter with the snow blowing in through the cracks of the privy."

Jen, at last, had a place of her own when Maybelle moved into Gram's room. She enjoyed having a closet to herself, the luxury of a double bed, the delicious sense of privacy. Yet when she dropped in to see her sister installed in her new quarters, it made her feel queer to see everything rearranged and tidy. "Where's the crazy quilt?"

"That ratty old thing? Back in the blanket box. Mama gave me the Apple Orchard instead." Proudly Maybelle smoothed out one of Gram's original creations: bright red apples on green trees patterned against a field of white. Jen thought of the gift her grandmother had started on her birthday. One day she would finish it, but right now it was the crazy quilt she wanted on her bed. Its comfort, she soon discovered, made up for the warm curl of Maybelle that was missing in the night.

Puss no longer cared to sit in the cane-backed rocker. Stiff-legged and ancient, she prowled about the house and yard as if in search of some remembered warm-blooded thing. Haughtily she stared down death with yellow eyes until one autumn night when she quietly disappeared.

"Oh, but I miss that dratted cat," Mama said again and again. All of them missed the animal's cool disdain, her sinuous flirtations when she needed to be stroked, but Rock took her departure happily in stride by moving into her favorite place behind the stove.

Luke's story, "A Walk on Main Street," was published in the October issue of the *Addison Review*. This was an obscure publication few people in town had ever heard of, and it might have gone unnoticed if Thomas O'Connell hadn't proudly loaned his copy to Miss Barrett who had, in turn, showed it excitedly to the high-school principal. Within a week Aurora was in an uproar. It was, as Eustace Bean put it bluntly, "as if Luke McAlister had pulled up a curtain on the town and showed us stark naked to the world."

Luke was astonished by the reaction. He had invented a place similar to the one he had grown up in, he insisted, and peopled it with imaginary characters, and he couldn't imagine what all the fuss was about. Unfortunately no one who read the story quite believed him. The general opinion was that Harry Shomers was in it plain as life and Rheba Watson and Mayor Willie Virkus and at least half a dozen local characters, with only the names changed around.

Papa had mixed feelings. "Son, I'm proud of your achievement, but didn't it ever occur to you that people might see themselves in that story and get mad?"

"I made up the characters from bits and pieces of a lot of people," Luke defended himself. "That's how writers write."

"But you've offended a lot of nice, decent folk, Luke. They think you were making fun of them."

Luke sighed and refused to talk about it anymore, but his triumph was spoiled. Yet the one most pained was his mother. The little scandal caused by "A Walk on Main Street" caused her deep and bitter distress. Not only were certain characters recognizable, but her son had described plainly certain matters that respectable citizens would blush to see in print. It cut even deeper when Ella remarked that she had read the story months ago and had encouraged Luke to submit it because she thought it was "such a good yarn." If that was the case, Mama wondered what the younger generation was coming to. And when she learned that the *Addison Review* had asked for another, she went to bed with a crushing migraine headache.

Jen read "A Walk on Main Street" several times. At first it was hard to separate the words from the author, but eventually she understood that her brother hadn't intended to ridicule anyone. It was quite unlike the romantic and sentimental stories in the popular magazines, and she respected Luke's ability to bring people to life in a way that seemed honest and true. Yet her anger toward him was so deep, the distance between them was so wide, that she could never say the words that would let him know how much she admired his work.

28

Ella Makes Plans

"How come I never see Mr. Shomers in here anymore?" Jen asked on an October afternoon when she stopped in at the store.

"He doesn't feel comfortable," her father said.

"Too bad for him, then!" Ella thumped a bolt of calico back on the shelf. "And I say good riddance."

"You insulted him," Papa accused her. "He's been dealing here for over fifty years, and now he's decided to take his business somewhere else."

"Business? Hah! If that's what you call all that coughing and spitting and fouling the air with his evil cigar. Let him try and finagle free smokes someplace else for a change."

"Why don't you walk on home with Jen?" Papa was brusque. "I'm sure I can manage without you until closing time."

A warm, honey light fell across the autumn fields, brightening the rich mix of goldenrod and wild asters that crowded up to the side of the road. "Is something wrong at the store?" Jen was sorry she had tipped over a row. Lately Ella and her father had been short with each other, but she had never heard them quarrel before.

"I'm thinking of leaving Aurora."

Jen was so taken by surprise she didn't know what to say.

"I've been offered another job over in Pendleton," Ella explained. "Modeling at the corset factory."

"Ella, you wouldn't!"

"Why wouldn't I? Ten dollars a week is nothing to sneeze at. Besides, it's perfectly respectable."

"Mama won't think so."

"It's my life, not hers. And there are other reasons for leaving."

"I hope I'm not one of them. I'm sorry for what I said to you this summer. I only did it because I guessed how Luke felt about you." It was good to get bad feelings out into the open.

Ella walked quickly in silence, then abruptly stopped. "I can't explain to you how or why it happened . . . but I want you to know that I care very much for your brother. That bothers you a lot, doesn't it?"

"Yes." Jen was truthful. "But I don't want you to go away. Neither will Mama."

"Oh, Jen." Ella walked on again. "She gave me advantages she never had . . . She's been mother and sister to me and *now* . . . That's why your father is angry with me. He knows how she'll feel if I take away the thing she prizes the most."

"Papa knows?"

"I'm sure he suspects. He can see that I'm wretched."

Jen had worried so much that she had to ask: "Or is he jealous of the two of you?"

"Oh, no! You must never think that. Maybe James loves

youth and romance, but he doesn't love me, at least not in that way." She asked Jen, "What else *can* I do but leave?"

"Tell Mama."

"I can't! She'd hate me! I've let her down before, Jen . . . I can't do it again."

"Please tell her. It will all come out in the wash."

Ella gave a sad little laugh. "Now isn't that just what Louisa would say? But you're wrong, Jen. It will never work out if I stay."

The uproar over Luke's story subsided in November as Election Day drew near. There was excited discussion about the outcome.

"Life has been good to us under President McKinley," Mama told the family one night at dinner. "Comfortable and prosperous. I can't say I care for that boisterous Theodore Roosevelt, but I don't suppose having him as Vice President will make a particle of difference." As a woman she couldn't vote herself, but she hoped that for once in his life her husband would see the light and vote for the solid Republican candidate. Instead, Papa traveled to the county seat where he sat on a hard bench for two hours while William Jennings Bryan, the silver-voiced Democrat, spoke compellingly against imperialism and the domination of the trusts. But it was Luke who annoyed both his parents with his enthusiasm for Eugene Debs, the leader of the Socialist Democratic Party.

"He cares about the working people who have built up

the wealth and power of this country by their blood and their sweat!" Luke pounded his fist on the table. "He believes in the public ownership of utilities, in distributing profits among all the people instead of letting them accumulate in the hands of a powerful few. And that's how I feel, too."

Mama told him that she suspected Thomas O'Connell had planted these dangerous notions in his head and that she hoped by the time he was old enough to vote he would have outgrown such revolutionary nonsense. When William McKinley was safely reelected, she was relieved to be able to turn her thoughts to the Thanksgiving preparations.

For weeks every child in the village had kept an eye on the weather, but except for a few faint flurries that melted before they touched the ground there had been nothing in the way of a real snowfall. Jen woke every day and glanced hopefully from her window for the first bright strokes of winter. Yet she loved the colors of November: green, gold, russet, purple, bursts of bittersweet abrupt and rich against the fading year. On Thanksgiving morning the snow came at last, frosting trees and bushes into dazzling confectionary shapes. It was well below freezing. Charles brought in a plentiful supply of firewood to keep the cookstove glowing hot, and then escaped to lie down in the whiteness of the yard, flapping his arms and legs to form the outline of an angel in the snow.

"Why, Jen!" Mama called from the dining room. "Did you make this centerpiece?"

In the fall Jen had gathered papery bundles of orange

Chinese lanterns and fragile stalks of silver dollar plants to make an arrangement for the table. "Yes. Do you like it?"

"It's very nice indeed." Jen was surprised that such a simple thing had given her mother pleasure.

All morning the house seemed to swell with the plump, golden odor of the roasting bird and the spicy fragrance of the pumpkin pies. As they sat down to dinner at one o'clock, Jen remembered how Gram had enjoyed each festive holiday meal.

"Let us give thanks." Papa bent his head above his folded hands. "Thank you, O Lord, on this Thanksgiving Day for the bounty of the harvest spread before us at this table. Let us be reminded of our many blessings in our beloved land and of the freedom and prosperity we enjoy under our most sacred flag. For all these things we are humbly grateful."

"And for snow," Charles prompted.

"For the pristine beauty of the first snowfall . . ." Papa smiled at his younger son, "and for the wonder it brings that makes us all children at heart."

"Amen." Charles, afraid that his father might get carried away, was anxious to finish the grace.

"Isn't it nice to think that people everywhere are sitting down to big fat feasts?" Maybelle said.

"Not everywhere." Luke mounded potatoes high on his plate and then poured on hot gravy. "In lots of places families won't be having anything at all."

Charles looked worried. "No turkey?"

"No turkey, no cranberries, no stuffing — "

"*Lukas* . . ." Ella placed a light, restraining hand on his wrist.

"It doesn't hurt to be reminded," Luke said, "that in cities like Chicago and New York thousands of poor immigrants are packed into filthy tenements, and that plenty of men, women, and children work ten hours a day, six days a week for a mere pittance."

"It doesn't help," Mama said, "to ruin a hard-earned holiday with gloomy socialistic talk."

"May I remind you, son," Papa put in, "that those poor huddled masses will one day find the same opportunities as the rest of us."

"The Lord helps those who help themselves," Mama said.

"Hungry people need more than ambition and motivation," Luke argued. "They need some tangible assistance — and legislation to prevent them from being exploited."

"Luke, I did not invite Mr. Debs to our Thanksgiving dinner," Mama told him, "and I'll thank you to please change the subject."

"I'll change it," Jen said. "Our class is going to put on an operetta in the spring, and I'm in charge of painting all the scenery."

"Scenery?" Maybelle made a face. "I'd rather sing songs and be the star."

"Nobody will ever get *me* on a stage," Charles announced. "I'd rather take castor oil."

"I have some news . . ." Ella passed the pan rolls down the table. "I've been offered a job at the Spiranna over in Pendleton."

Luke held the plate suspended in midair. "Doing what?"

"Modeling corsets in the factory."

Mama's face flushed. "I won't hear of it!"

"Now, it's decent work." Ella lifted her chin. "And it isn't as if we parade down the street in our stays. There's even a comfortable boarding house nearby where I can live inexpensively. I've imposed on you long enough."

"What's imposed?" Charles asked.

"She means she's been a nuisance," Maybelle told him.

"You've been more than welcome here, Ella." Papa had stopped eating. "I hope it isn't something I've done that's made you unhappy."

"It isn't you, James." Ella quickly put a hand over his. "This is just something I have to do."

"You can't go." Luke spoke quietly. "We won't let you."

"Lukas, you can't stop me." Ella looked around the table at the troubled faces. "I've made up my mind, and I'm leaving."

29

Two Eventful Nights

Deep in the cold November dark the fire bell rang and rang. Jen, under a warm hive of covers, wakened briefly to its brassy clatter and heard noises below — the front door slamming shut, horses pounding past along the road. In the morning she first smelled smoke and then remembered.

Mama was in the kitchen, looking out the window. "There's been the most terrible fire."

"Not the store!"

"No, thank God for that. It's the Eldorado. Mr. Riley tells me that it's gone. I can't believe that it's burned to the ground."

Vanished? In one night? Jen, looking at the thick dark haze downriver, couldn't believe it either. "I have to go and see."

"I'll go with you. First make yourself tidy."

"Not now. It doesn't matter."

"It always matters," Mama insisted.

In the village everyone was outdoors. Shocked and pleasurably excited, people stood in small humming knots; children ran about shouting to their friends and dogs barked hoarsely around the edges of the disaster. Where the graceful white edifice had stood, firemen dragged hoses through the smoking remains. Nothing was left but a scrawl of stinking beams and charred timbers, ruined chairs and beds and tables, soaked mattresses, smashed crockery.

"Luke!" Jen, picking her way around the debris, caught sight of her brother. "Have you been here all night?"

"Most of it." His eyes were stained red from smoke and fatigue and there was a long streak of blood on his cheek. He said hopelessly, "We tried to save it, but we didn't have a chance in that wind."

Frozen water flowered grotesquely from broken window frames and blackened latticework. "I always thought that growing up was dancing at the Eldorado." Jen was bleak.

"You'll dance somewhere else, little sister."

"Go home, son." Eustace Bean clapped Luke wearily on the shoulder. There were splinters of ice in his beard. "You've done all that you can do for now."

"I'll be glad to stay on for a while."

"Come back later when you've eaten and had some rest." The fire captain's boots crunched away. It was snowing, hard grainy pellets that stung the cheeks. Ella ran toward them, her light hair spilling out from under her heavy hat. Her hand touched the cut on Luke's face. "Are you all right?"

"I'm fine. I'm going home to get some sleep."

"Then I'll go along and fix some breakfast for you."

"You've had a bad night." Papa had arrived with the younger children. "How's Mr. Hammond taking it?"

"Hard," Luke said. "He says he's too old to rebuild."

"That's a pity then. I hate to see a fine old landmark disappear."

Later Jen learned from her mother that Willard Roth was in bed with the chicken pox. Knowing how he would have enjoyed a catastrophe firsthand, she was very glad he had missed it.

It was almost midnight and she couldn't sleep or stop thinking about the fire, about the wind greedily lapping up the wild orange flames and a million sparks sucked up and whirled away. Awful and yet gorgeous, too, in a terrible way. Rumors were already going around that Mr. Hammond had been offered an enormous sum, that someone wanted to build a pickle factory on the site. Jen couldn't imagine summer without the sunlit porches of the Eldorado and the city guests arriving, emanating glamour like heady perfume.

Outside an owl fluted softly in the darkness. The sound called to something lonesome in her. She got out of bed and knelt by the window, wondering where the owl might be. There was a faint bloom of snow in the yard, the river a silver streak beyond. Along the riverbank black branches climbed a glowing wall of winter night.

If only she had someone to talk to. Ella might welcome company. She had been different at supper — warmer and softer, the way she used to be. Maybe Luke had persuaded her not to leave after all. Jen hoped so. How flat and uninteresting, how colorless everything would seem without her. She would go and tell Ella that now.

The room down the hall was empty, the bedding un-rumpled. Jen slipped down the stairs without a sound. The parlor door was shut, the kitchen in darkness. Behind the stove Rock tapped his tail faintly and then sighed himself back to sleep. In the dining room, coals still glowed red through the isinglass window of the base burner. Worried, Jen wondered if her brother would know where Ella was. He was still up; there was a thread of yellow shining under his door. As she came closer she heard the murmur of voices and realized that Ella was there, talking to Luke. What if Mama came down and discovered them together!

Quickly she retraced her steps. In bed she rolled into a ball and drew her knees against her chest. Something was going on that she didn't understand. Gradually, as the minutes passed and the old house creaked in the frosty night, she began to relax.

She was wakened by a light tug at the covers. "Who is it?"

"Shhhhhhh." The room was iced with moonlight. Jen saw a shadowy presence, a cloudy plume of breath, and smelled the familiar scent of rose geranium. "Please, honey . . . don't make a sound."

"What's wrong?"

Ella sat down on the side of the bed. Jen saw the dark flare of her hat, the trim shape of her coat. "I've come to say good-bye."

"You're going now? In the middle of the night?" Jen twisted to look at the clock. "At a quarter to four?"

"Listen to me. Lukas and I are taking the early train to New York."

"You *and* Luke. But why?"

"We love each other, and we want to live together. I know it must seem cowardly, our running away like this, but it really is the only way."

"Then you're going to be married?"

"Jen, I've been married." Ella hesitated, then went on. "Neither of us wants that right now. And of course your parents won't understand."

"*I* don't understand."

"All I can tell you is that Lukas and I need to be together now."

"But when are you coming back?"

"We can't . . . unless we decide to marry. Otherwise, you know it would be impossible."

"You mean I might never see either of you again?"

"Oh, honey . . . no tears." Ella touched her gloved fingers to Jen's cheek. "Of course we'll see you *someday.* Perhaps, later on, you'll even come to visit us in New York. You'd like that, wouldn't you? So you mustn't fret about it now. Please don't be angry with us. We're both very happy, you see." Her laughter was low and contented. "Wish us luck."

"I do . . . of course, I do. But what about Mama?"

"We'll be in touch just as soon as we can. In the meantime you'll have to explain this to your mother the best way you can." Ella pulled Jen close and kissed her, and quickly left the room.

There was another shadow at the door, and then Luke stood by the bed. "Ella's told you?"

"Yes." Jen pulled the crazy quilt around herself to try to stop her shivering. "But why do you have to go like this?"

"I need to," Luke said. "I have to find out what is so particular about this village . . . this house . . . this family. And I think I'll only understand what it means when I write about it somewhere else."

"Why do you want to write about ordinary people like us?"

"Because you're *my* family . . . and that makes you *extra*ordinary," he said. "You'll be the oldest now, and that's not easy. I ought to know. I've done some stupid and cruel things."

"You made me hate Papa."

"You can love him again if you try."

"I can't! It's too hard. I can never forget what you said."

"It will be easier if you're kind — " His soft mustache brushed against her lips. "And you are."

"Luke—wait!" She caught hold of his coat sleeve. "That story you wrote . . . it was so fine! I know you'll write others just as good."

"Better ones, Jen." He held her briefly and then was gone. She didn't hear footsteps on the stairs, only a furtive bump of sound as the front door closed behind them. She imagined them walking side by side down the River Road under the wide, amazed eye of the moon and felt a deep excitement, as if the fierce, charged force connecting them had given her a sudden, breathless shock.

What they were doing was selfish and wrong. She knew it. They should have had the courage to tell Mama and Papa what they had said to her. She loved them, but they now seemed smaller in her eyes. She didn't want to think about the morning, when she would have to break the news.

From her pillow Jen saw a bright metallic scattering of stars. She had never felt more alone. Nothing was safe or settled or secure. Only the very young believed that, and her childhood was as remote to her now as the cool points of light, immeasurably distant.

The Sound of Bells

December trembled with the sound of bells, of brass and bronze and silver, of church bells chiming the familiar carols, of sleigh bells dancing down the glistening roads and icy village streets. It was endlessly cascading snow, noisy school concerts, a nativity pageant staged at Pickwick Hall with an angelic Charles flapping celestial, wired-on wings. A month briskly in motion with people dressing up and going out and coming home again, high-spirited, in cutters. Jen, who couldn't fall in step this year, felt a numb wonder at others who could.

There was comfort and safety in rituals. There was the usual spell of planning, of dreaming, of secret whispered consultations between the younger children. Mama made her rich dark fruitcakes, soaked them in brandy, and set them aside to ripen in two-pound honey tins. At night she stayed up late when the others were in bed, putting neat finishing touches to shirts and chemises, straining her eyes over delicate hand-embroidery, but she lacked the vitality of other years. Jen supervised the construction of the paper chains, the red and green strips of paper looped together and sealed with flour-and-water paste. She made batches of popcorn and threaded festive necklaces for the tree, with a cranberry winking between each snowy kernel, but it was a chore this time, not a pleasure.

On nights when McAlister's was open late and Papa stayed in town, she sat with her mother at home, slumped over Latin and algebra while Mama worked at knitting or sewing. There were sudden little sounds; fire hissed and fluttered in the base burner and the old house creaked in the wind like a rocking ship, but they seldom spoke. When her homework was finished, Jen would go down to the cold cellar and bring up a pan of russet apples to mellow by the stove. Sometimes she would ask, "Would you like me to read to you, Mama?" but the answer was rarely yes. Usually her mother said, with a negative shake of the head, "I think not, tonight," and Jen would understand that it had been another difficult day.

Only once did the silent woman speak of what was troubling her. Raising her eyes from the needles that angrily snapped at each other in her flashing hands, she said, "I loved them both so dearly . . . Why can't I bear the thought of the two of them together?" The girl, startled by the wondering pain in her voice, came quickly to the chair, dropped to her knees, put her head into her mother's lap. "You have *me!* You still have me!"

Mama pulled back, tried to push her away. "Get up, Jen. That's enough . . . Why, a great big girl like you!"

"Why can't I touch you? Why won't you ever touch me?"

Her face awry with panic, Mama said, "You know that's all nonsense. I'm sure I don't know what you're talking about. Look, now . . . you've spilled the wool."

Quickly Jen picked up the colored balls of yarn, returned

to the table and bent over her books, a hand shading her brimming eyes. Out of the shining jumble of algebraic symbols in front of her one cold fact emerged. The strange lack in her mother, the deep need in herself, would not be resolved. Never again would she offer what wouldn't be taken or ask for what couldn't be given. Growing up, Davey had told her, was seeing things as they are. Now she did. The difference between herself and her father was that he still hoped that Mama would change. Jen's anger toward him was gone, replaced by pity for his childish dream.

A bronchial cough kept her mother at home, and a few days before Christmas Jen went alone to an evening carol service at St. John's. Flowers were banked at the altar and tall white tapers spilled a flickering light around the holy crèche.

> *"O come all ye faithful,*
> *Joyful and triumphant,*
> *O come ye, O come ye, to Bethlehem."*

The junior choir advanced in pairs, cupping candles in their hands. Charles had forgotten to take out his gum, and he sang and chewed exuberantly, both at the same time.

> *"Come and behold Him,*
> *Born the king of angels . . ."*

Now the adult choir in crimson cassocks followed the children up the center aisle, the stronger, richer voices with the higher and sweeter soaring to the aged rafters.

> *"O come let us adore Him,*
> *O come let us adore Him . . ."*

An inner music in Jen responded to the lush ascending notes.

> *"O come let us adore Him,*
> *Christ the Lord!"*

Beauty was everywhere: in burnished brass, the scarlet petals of the poinsettias, the exultation of the singers. It was Christmas. At last she was touched by the joyful spirit of the celebration.

The Yule tree had always been Luke's responsibility. Each year the children dogged after him in the snow, shouting and pointing out dozens of prospects until eventually he found the biggest broadest bushiest best and cut it down. This year Eustace Bean, intending to be kind, dropped off a magnificent spruce from his woodlot, but Jen, seeing how disappointed Charles and Maybelle were, promised that next year they would go again and find their own.

On the Saturday before Christmas she took them with her to the village. Streets were hung with evergreen, shop windows were bright with tinsel, and the big jars of colored water in the window of the pharmacy glowed like gigantic ornaments. Outside the saloon a tall figure heavily bundled against the cold stood ringing a cowbell and begging for alms for the needy.

"I wish I had some money." Maybelle spoke loud enough for Mrs. Watson to hear. "If I did I'd give it all to the poor."

"You would not."

"I would so, Charles."

"Now stop that." Jen gave their mittened hands a shake. "I'm sure Maybelle means what she says."

All along the Brick Block friends and neighbors, red faces warm with smiles, stopped to speak and send greetings home, but nobody mentioned Luke or Ella. Only Thomas O'Connell brought the subject out into the open. "Any word from your brother, Jen?"

"Not yet."

"Your mother must be taking this hard. I know your father is."

"Yes, sir."

"I miss Luke. He's a bright, hard-working young man, and I certainly wish him well. We haven't heard the last of him . . . I'm sure that he'll make us all proud someday. Will you tell your mother I was asking for her?"

"I will."

"Wait a minute, sonny." The lawyer waved his hands and tweaked Charles by the nose. "That's an odd place to keep your spending money."

"I don't have any money."

"Then what's this?" Mr. O'Connell handed the boy a shining silver dollar.

Charles gasped. "That came out of my nose?"

"You too, Maybelle . . . and Jen." The clever fingers flashed again and again, producing two more gleaming coins.

"Thank you, Mr. O'Connell! Merry Christmas!"

Beaming, they watched the lawyer head down the street toward Dewey's.

"All right, Maybelle." Charles gleefully pointed toward Rheba Watson, who was still ringing the cowbell. "You said that you would if you could. Now you can."

Maybelle only clutched her silver dollar tighter. "I'm going to hang on to it awhile."

All along the street Charles tugged hopefully at his nose, but the magic had disappeared with Mr. O'Connell.

There was a holiday bustle in the general store. It was the time of year when customers were expected to settle their accounts in all the shops, but everyone knew that Jamie McAlister was lenient. Instead of badgering his debtors he invited the men to drink some Christmas cheer and treated their wives and children to cookies and candy. Jen had promised to help out during the afternoon; as she weighed cheese and ground coffee beans she kept an eye out for Davey. He had promised to stop in and say goodbye before he went home to the farm.

Little Miss Hutchins popped out from the post office and cocked her head, looking at Jen with her bright birdy eyes. "Young Sawyer was in here this morning looking for you. Good-looking lad, he is."

"Did he say if he'd be back?"

"Didn't say. Is he your sweetheart, Jen?"

She didn't have to answer. Mr. Shomers shuffled in for the first time in weeks, wearing a shabby, rumpled coat, a battered hat, and torn overshoes, like a man back from a violent journey. He aimed for the spittoon and missed, then stood peering into the case next to the register. Finally he pointed. "I'll take that one." It was *not* the last cigar in the box. For once he was willing to pay, to give up his little game. With a smile Jen handed him the best one she could find. "It's free, Mr. Shomers," she told him. "Merry Christmas!"

It was late afternoon when Papa told her to go home.

"Can't I stay until closing?"

"No, I promised your mother you'd all be home by suppertime. She wants you to pick up some of her cough medicine at Ulbrich's."

Jen collected the children and slowly headed for the pharmacy.

"My sister wants to give you something!" Charles called to the woman ringing the bell outside the saloon.

"Stop pushing, Charles."

Maybelle stared hard and long at the coin in her hand. Then with a sigh she dropped it into the big iron kettle.

"Bless you, child!" cried Rheba Watson.

"That was a very unselfish thing to do," Jen said as they went on their way. "And I'm going to buy you both an ice cream soda."

"I'll have chocolate." Maybelle looked a little brighter.

"I want I-don't-care." That was what Charles loved best,

a mixture made from all the odds and ends of flavored syrups.

There was a special fascination to the drugstore, with its penetrating medicinal odor and strange therapeutic contraptions. There were hundreds of little drawers filled with roots and herbs and hundreds of little bottles filled with potent concoctions guaranteed to cure every human ill. At the back of the store was the exotic splendor of the soda fountain with its cool streaked marble counter, shining nickel-plated taps, and sensuous pyramids of polished glasses.

"Jen! Did you see Davey Sawyer? He was just in here looking for you." It was Mary Frances, waiting for Mr. Ulbrich to wrap a bottle of Dr. Pierce's Golden Medical Discovery. Friends again, now that Willard was pursuing Jessamine Doyle, the girls chatted briefly, and then Jen handed her silver dollar over to her sister. "You two go ahead and have your sodas. And wait for me here . . . I'll be right back."

Outside, the village shone with the fine porcelain glow of early winter. Walking briskly, Jen searched both sides of the street, but by the time she reached the place where the white hotel had stood she was convinced she had missed seeing Davey. The Eldorado had been especially beautiful at Christmas, with candles lit in every window and ragged bursts of pine boughs on the double doors. Now snow was heaped softly over the ruins, the pale shrouded shapes reminding her of furniture stored under dustcloths until another season. There was a rumor that Mr. Hammond might rebuild in the spring. She hoped it was true.

Hands were clapped over her ears from behind. She pried them away and whirled around. "Davey!"

"Am I glad to see you." He had a dark cap pulled low over his forehead. "My folks have kept me busy most of the day. By the time I got back to McAlister's you'd already left. I was sure that I'd missed you."

"And I've been looking everywhere for you." They stood close together, breath smoking white in the frosty dark.

"How are things at home now?" he asked.

"Cold." Jen pushed up the collar of her coat. "With Luke and Ella gone the rooms feel empty. It's quiet. Sad."

"I know. It was like that when my brother died. Everyone so polite. I wanted to kick over chairs and smash things, but I didn't. That's when I started thinking about everything, making plans."

"What kind of plans?"

"About what to do with my life. I know I won't be staying on the farm. I'd like to go on to some big university . . . maybe study medicine or law . . . but there might be something else I haven't thought of yet." He asked, "What about you, Jen? What do you want?"

No one had ever asked her that before. Women stayed home and got married and reared children. Or was it possible that they had choices, too?

She wanted so much. Love, laughter, joy . . . she was Gram's girl, wasn't she? Yet she wanted even more than that. To seize a moment, color it, create something beautiful of her own, that was what mattered most. She didn't tell him that. She would never tell anyone that. Instead she said gaily, "I intend to do a lot of dancing, Davey."

Her scarf blew across his face. He tugged at one end and pulled her against him. His lips were warm as he kissed her. Jen kissed him back. Hugged him, hard.

"You're strong!" He grinned. "I mean, *really* strong."

"Yes, I am." Laughing, she thought of Madame Bonnomo's exercises. "I've been working at it."

They stood before dawn in the clean green fragrance of the parlor staring at the shining beauty of the tree. Then they attacked the stockings hanging by the fireplace, lumpy with secrets. Nuts and red mesh bags of satiny-striped hard candy and chocolate doubloons wrapped in glittering foil, like a pirate's golden treasure. Last of all, in the toe, the rare, sweet pleasure of a Christmas orange. Rock, bewildered by the rustle and commotion, raced around and around the room and then sat up and tipped his head for treats.

"Give him something," Maybelle said.

"Bad for his teeth." Charles's mouth was stuffed full.

Jen, the familiar excitement building in her chest, remembered how Gram had always been the first one up on Christmas morning.

Mama insisted that everyone have breakfast before the gifts were opened. She had set the dining-room table the night before with the best cutwork cloth and the pink-and-white china. Fire sang and sparkled behind the isinglass window of the stove as she brought in the platters of ham and eggs and bacon, and the fresh holiday stollen. "Charles, you must eat something."

He squirmed and jiggled in his chair. "I just did. All the candy in my stocking."

"I mean something sensible." Mama stood with the blue enamelware pot poised in the air. "Coffee, Jen?"

"You mean me? Yes, please!"

"I want some, too."

Mama said, "Your turn will come, Maybelle."

The rich dark brew arced expertly into the cup, filling it halfway. Papa, with an odd smile, pushed across the pressed glass creamer and sugar bowl. It was the old wind-flower pattern, passed along the table for years, but special on this day because it had stopped at Jen's place.

"Coffee stunts your growth," Maybelle said. "I read that in a book."

"I don't mind," Jen told her. "I'm tired of growing, anyway."

"*And* keeps you awake all night."

"But sleeping is such a waste of time." Jen lifted the cup to her lips. Everyone was watching her. She took a sip and swallowed noisily.

"How is it?" Charles asked.

She would never admit that it was disappointing, even disagreeable. It was the privilege that mattered, not the taste. "Absolutely dee — licious!"

After breakfast the gifts were exchanged in the parlor: the bay rum aftershave, handmade bookmarks and pen-wipers, the shirts and chemises and mufflers and mittens. A tucked shirtwaist for Jen with a high ruffled collar and bands of delicate embroidery. She knew the hours of care-ful work it had taken, time doubly precious to a woman with so little of it. "Mama, I love it. It's so beautiful." Jen's gift from her father was a tiny package of scent. "Rose geranium." With a pang she was reminded of Ella.

If only she could look up to him and trust him again, but she didn't know how. Her eyes went to the piano, to the wedding photographs linked by the golden hinge. With shortcomings and failures on both sides, some deep enduring bond held her parents together. Maybe loving *in spite of* took a special generosity of spirit, a certain courage.

His smile was tentative. "You can change it for anything you want."

She unstopped the bottle and inhaled, touched a few drops to her wrists. One day she would choose her own particular fragrance, Like Tiger Lily, maybe, Or Purple Passion Orchids. "It smells lovely, Papa. Thank you. It's exactly right."

Maybelle was delighted with a bouquet of colored hair ribbons from her sister and Charles ecstatic with a toy boomerang, although Jen wondered, as it sailed wildly around the parlor, if she might not soon regret having given it. Her gift to her parents was the last one to be unwrapped. She was nervous as Mama unhurriedly removed the paper and smoothed it neatly to be used another time.

The woman sat staring at a portfolio of sketches that Jen had done throughout the year and hidden under the nightgowns in her bottom drawer. There were dozens of them, some in crayon, others in pastels or watercolors: the family drinking the New Year's toast, Maybelle setting the table, Gram piecing the sunburst quilt and brushing her long silver hair at night, There was Ella in the red shawl,

Warner grimly stitching, Mama trussing the Thanksgiving turkey, Papa delivering the Decoration Day address.

Papa glanced through them, lingering over one of Luke grooming his mustache and a radiant Ella coming down the stairs on Memorial Day. "These are charming, dear. You've reminded us what an eventful year it's been."

"You could have done me smiling," Maybelle complained.

Charles laughed at a sketch of himself buried deep in bright autumn leaves with only the top of his head sticking out.

Mama took a long time sorting through the pictures. Some she held up to the light, others she studied silently in her lap. Finally she carried them with her into the kitchen.

Jen followed. Her mother, holding the package against her breast, stood staring remotely out the window.

"You don't like them, do you?" It hurt to have failed again.

Mama turned and Jen saw that she was deeply moved. "You couldn't have given me anything that I'd appreciate more." Her voice was full of emotion. Quickly she brushed at her eyes. "I don't know much about art — but I do know that these are wonderful pictures! It's as if you've captured time!"

"They aren't that good."

"Yes, they are. You have a gift. I should have paid more attention," Mama said. "Maybe one day you'll have your chance . . . I mean go to some important place to study. We'll have to give it some thought and do what we can."

Was it possible that someone, so practical and so predictable was saying such wild and improbable things? Elated, Jen flew across the room to throw her arms around her mother's neck.

"Now that's enough! If we don't hurry we'll all be late for church."

The table still seemed too large for the five of them. Maybelle had set two extra places. "Maybe Luke and Ella will come."

"Not today." Mama removed the extra plates and silverware. "Perhaps another time."

Papa uncorked the cider with a bright little pop. "Shall we have our Christmas toast?" Carefully he filled the goblets all around, then stood for a time without speaking, thinking of what he would say. Jen knew it would be a lengthy speech, the last of the year.

"To all of us . . ." He raised his arm and smiled. "To Mama, Jen, Maybelle, and Charles . . . and to those who are absent today but are with us in spirit." Gently he touched his glass to each of theirs. "May we always be kind to those we love."

It was a good toast, Jen thought. The simplest and the best. All of them drank except Mama, who was lost in thought as she watched the golden bubbles rush upward.

"Pretty Girl?" Her husband came to stand beside her. "You'll drink with us, won't you?"

Startled, she looked at all of them, then took a tiny ritual sip.

"Good. That's done then." Impulsively he kissed her. Mama's hand rose to her cheek in the familiar gesture of dismissal, but this time it stopped in midair and fell back to her side.

"Girls, let's get the dinner on the table before it gets cold."

This year when the coffee was served after dinner, Jen decided, she would fill her own cup to the brim.